there were many horses

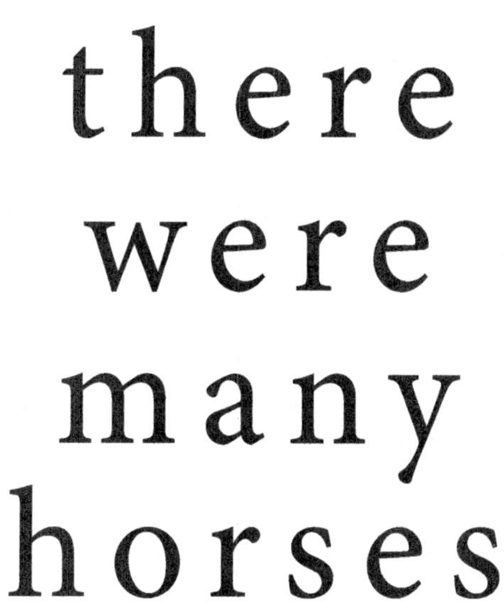

Luiz Ruffato

Translated by
Anthony Doyle

amazoncrossing

Previously published as *Eles eram muitos cavalos* in 2001 in Brazil. Translated from Portuguese by Anthony Doyle. First published in English by AmazonCrossing in 2014.

Published by AmazonCrossing, Seattle

www.apub.com

ISBN-13: 9781477819524
ISBN-10: 1477819525

Cover design by David Drummond

Library of Congress Control Number: 2013919546

Printed in the United States of America

They were so many horses
but no one remembers their names,
their coats, their origin . . .

CECÍLIA MEIRELES

How long will you defend the unjust
and show partiality to the wicked?

PSALM 82

1. Dateline

São Paulo, May 9, 2000.
Tuesday.

2. The Weather

In the state capital today the sky will vary from overcast to cloudy.
Temperature — Low: 14°; High: 23°.
Air quality regular to good.
Sunrise at 6:42 a.m.; sunset at 5:27 p.m.
Crescent moon.

3. Hagiology

Saint Catherine of Bologna, born in Ferrara, Italy, in 1413, was Superioress at a convent in Bologna. On Christmas Day, 1456, she received the infant Jesus from the hands of Our Lady. She devoted her life to the needy and saw the fulfillment of God's will as her sole vocation. She died in 1463.

4. En route

The Neon speeds along the irregular asphalt, ignoring the creases, bumps, grooves, potholes, saliences, ridges, pebbles, black nooks in the black night, imprisoned, the hypnotic music, tum-tum tum-tum, conducts his rocking trunk, tum-tum tum-tum, sensual hands caress the leather of the steering wheel, tum-tum tum-tum, the body, the car, they plow ahead, abducting the lights that glare left and right, a ring bought on the Portobello Road, a satellite on the right-hand ring finger, tum-tum, tum-tum, the bolide hurtles toward Cumbica Airport, rushing headlong through the headlights of buses converging from all sides,

more schmucks to screw over

five-foot eleven *is on the army enlistment papers*, Giorgio Armani shirt and pants, a splash of Polo cologne, Italian shoes, clean-shaven, hair sheared at grade two, gold Rolex under the cuff

more schmucks to screw over

she should be arriving by now, one of those stars that glide above the highway, the woman, the boss

Urgent business in brasília I explained to

yeah, sure, he treats him like

The son he wished he'd had

yeah, sure, ***the asshole***, cokemeister son who struts his arrogance about the brokerage.

yeah, sure, ***the asshole***, cokemeister son who parades his steroids round bartables and clubs—already bust—to bouncers and hookers—already bust—round typewriters at the precinct—already

yes but he's still my son
Bribing the cops,
the chief inspector,
the club owner,
the hookers,
the bouncers,
yes, but he's still my son
yeah, sure, the daughter lives in Embu, macrobiotic, an esoteric artist whose paintings are always the same
there are none so blind
red, hysterical, spasmodic, thick, fine slashes, white background
as will not see
I fucked her once *horrendous* in her studio, among brushes and paint tins on a large blank canvas stretched out on a table
this is art
she, the smell of incense,
marijuana is natural
naked under an Indian shawl, drops of semen on the white surface
this is art
more schmucks to screw over
she sulked *regretful?* in a corner, just a
hired hand
yes, but the father loves me
a competent professional
because I make him money on the stock exchange
a huge apartment in moema, one per floor, three suites *I hired one of those queens, money's not a problem, he goes to*

town, the chicks can't believe it, then I say the decor was by so-and-so and it makes them come
yes, competent:
six years ago he was slinking skinny through the sparse shade on the sad streets of muriaé, sad town
five years ago he was sprinkled with the first snowflakes of fairfield ohio thanks to an american fields scholarship won through a competition at the rotary club of muriaé, sad town
four years ago he was cutting his teeth at citibank
sinking those teeth in at citibank
for two years he's been earning money for
the old man won't leave me a goddam thing
for a year now he's been cooking the books at the brokerage
it'll all go to
she's arriving from london-gatwick, a ring purchased on the portobello road in the palm of her hand
it's yours
how was london?
tum-tum tum-tum tum-tum tum-tum

5. Off the top of the head

Here comes the trio, in single file, on the path by the roadside. Their bodies, dissolved into the dark, emerge briefly in the headlights of the trucks, buses, and cars feeling their way through the night. The three stomp through the bush, the tall grass scratching their trouser legs.

They are father, son, and another, known only by sight, who, with words of encouragement, *Sure you can, been doing it on foot for ten years now. Heck of a saving at the end of the month,* has decided to tag along.

The man drives a haystacker for a transporter in Limão.

The boy is ten-or-elevenish, though so skinny he looks even younger. He quit school to sell hot dogs—with ketchup or mayonnaise—and Coca-Cola outside the firm where his father works. He stores his cart there at night, in the patio, and the security guards look after it. When he grows up and is out on his own, he wants to be a trucker.

The other, unemployed, is up for anything, *It's a deal then!*

The lad walks on up front, the man in the middle, and the other bringing up the rear.

—This one here is worth his weight in gold, says the father, all proud, trying to glean the physiognomy of the other at his back, with his asthmatic rasp and eager, shuffling feet. Sharp as a tack! Watch this. He turns and checks the sign on a fast-approaching bus,

"Garanhuns," he spurts.

—Pernambuco, the boy responds, automatically. The other scoffs, "That's it?"

—He knows every town in Brazil, says the father. He has a map inside his head, the pest.

—Every town?

—Every last one!

The other, known only by sight, stops, turns, tries to read the place name off the speeding oncoming bus, but *Shit!* he misses it, *Too fast . . . Shit!* Embarrassed, he reaches for a name, *Alagoinhas,* the name of his hometown, "Alagoinhas." *He'll never get this one.*

—Bahia, says the boy, off the cuff.

—Is that right, Bahia? asks the father, at a push.

—Yep, says the other, vexed.

Without looking back, he waits for the next bus to come rattling along, "Itaberaba," his wife's hometown, *Now this time . . .* "Bahia, too." *The runt got it! The pipsqueak!*

—Told ya.

—Where the hell did he learn all that?

—Don't ask me. . . .

—Doesn't say much, does he? Hey, kid! Hey!

—Yeah . . . Not much of a talker . . . Shy as a rabbit . . .

Puffed, the father turns and glances at an oncoming bus, "Governador Valadares."

—Minas Gerais.

—Impressive! he has to admit. They trudge on, the grass blades pricking their arms.

—Ever thought of putting him on TV?

—Whassat?

—Yeah . . . those shows where people answer questions and stuff . . .

—Television?

Television . . .

Any cash in that?

—Tons!

The man watches his son marching on ahead, lost under a tawdry jacket two sizes too big

the buses trucks cars lights of São Paulo

Television . . .

6. Mother

The pop-eyed old woman clinging to seat number 3 on the Garanhuns–São Paulo intercity bus has not slept in forty-eight hours and is clutching the armrest trying to gauge the speed, *Good God, why so fast?* while hanging on the driver's every word as he shoots the breeze with acquaintances harvested from the asphalt, *Good God, he's not keeping his eyes on the road!* Devout, she prays and prays that the journey will end soon, as she can't even go to the restroom, what with being tossed about like this, and then there is the stench wafting from the cubicle down the back, there's just no way, despite her bursting bladder and runny tummy, *Good God!* she can only relieve herself on pit-stops, when the shake-and-rattle stops. *Are we nearly there yet?* **Patience, grandma! Still a ways to go**, sealed-in pestilent air, sweating window panes, scattered about the floor: popsicle sticks; plastic cups; plastic bottles; crumbs from tapioca biscuits, bread rolls, maize loaves; flour; leftovers; a baby-blue crocheted baby shoe, day-and-night, *And some people even manage to sleep, my God, croc-mouthed, snoring even! Dribbling! How on earth?* changing landscapes blend and fuse, huuuge cities flit by, and little towns go zoom! and they're gone,

&

Barbed-wire fences, billets, grass knolls, termite mounds, bull carcasses, buzzards, blue sky, snakes, crested seriemas, crested flycatchers, beetles, wheelie carts, horses, oxen, donkeys, mules, old boots, fens, eaves, goats, turds, roaches, critters, banana trees, bicycles, shrubs, trees, trees, trees

The engine humming in the inner ear (huuuummmm) (zuuuummmm)

&

Bush, fields, canefields, cables, brook, river, rivulet, rill, water-course, water, tannery, leather, horn, head, horseshoe, sundried meat, salt, dogs, spoons, knives, forks, glasses, plates, hand, smells, chimney, dogs, bush,

careful careful careful careful careful careful

pain, pangs, gifts, pain, pangs, pains, buildings, chimneys, fumes, cigarettes, smoke, flour, beans, fire, blazes, chickens, folks, goal-posts, football pitches, footballers, kits, colors fading on the washing line, hat, ball, bee, bile, cats, chickens, windows, jeeps, constrictors, windows, windows, wanderers, panic, piss, corpses, mounds, mountains, corpses, mounds, mountains, and

&

The engine humming in the inner ear (huuuummmm) *clouds, night, midnight, spade, foot, dust, backlands, bushtrails, rocks, rocks, rocks, bridges, plantations, rats, rags, drylands, drought, sun, silence, sum, sun sun sun sun hook, parched land, buzzards, imbus, buzzards, floodplains, greenery, gray, ash, the smell of*

careful careful careful careful careful careful

white cattle on green pasture, rock-desert cloud, dry clothes, dried meats, land, land, land, wind, green-hot day, blue-chill afternoon, night strewn with dusty stars, the world, bigoldworld, that never-ever ends and **Hey grandma, we're almost** bursting, so full it hurts, back pain, *Ouch!* the hips, *Ow!* the legs, *Ouch, ow,* no comfortable position, **See there grandma, the lights of São** son waiting for her *After all these years!* Went to make a life in Sampaulo, as for Brejo Velho, *Only came back twice, my God,* and that was when he was single, after that postcards brought the only news, job, girlfriend-now-wife, the pair of them, the detached house, her grandkids, so we look forward to you coming to spend Mother's Day with us and we will all be delighted and don't worry, I'll pick you up at the terminal, love to all in the exploding bladder, the runny tummy, how do you read through a son's eyes? Know if he's really happy at work, in marriage, if, *Ow!* the bladder, the belly, the back, *Ouch!* The hips, *Ai!* The legs, *Ouch! Ow!* no position left to sit in

At the terminal, on foot, she wrings her hands.

7. 66

The vibrations of today's number suggest success in the material aspects of life

(more money and prestige)

You may receive help

from an influential friend

You may receive a promotion

or inheritance:

now is a time to be practical

and objective.

8. There was a boy

A jesuschrist on his back like that doesn't even look like a child the long blond hair and beard old brown eyes a jesuschristy picture bought one sunny sunday at the fair in republica square a disgruntled kid getting his first taste of how things are a formidable kid a whiz at math and physics and chemistry an ace in Portuguese and taking advanced english at the local language school a marvelous lad with muscles toned from taekwondo an adorable boy pushing the supermarket cart for his mom amused by the way she dallies on the aisles calculator in hand adding and subtracting and multiplying and dividing until she muddles the total and seriously miffed quits checking prices weights expiration dates and just piles stuff into the cupboards and they sit down exhausted in the sitting room to watch the news with their plateful of lunch leftovers in the palms of their hands and their feet propped up on the coffee table and in those moments she feels attuned to some higher being in harmony with the positive forces of the universe and even forgives the man who left her with a kid to raise I need some time and the boy growing up without a father figure which could be a problem in the future some trauma in his head all these anxious worries and I don't mean to interfere son but this boy this boy is not good company for you ah the volcanic roil of adolescence and after work it was a double shift doing freelance jobs for magazines so that the lad could go to all the best places she wanted to give him that at least seeing as she failed dismally to provide him with a decent father who called every now and then to say how are things going and sorry I have to skip the check this month because things are pretty slow but next month I promise blah blah blah and when his birthday came around and it's hey champ and at christmas hey champ let's see if this year we don't go on vacation just you and me and good news I'm partner in

a communications consultancy I'm seriously thinking of applying for an Italian passport to go work in the EU, doing whatever, see
he remarried
became a city-hall shyster all that stuff in the papers none of it's true your mom's a journalist she knows it's all fabrication muckraking it makes me sick
got separated and shacked up with a chick of twentysomething pocked with cellulite no I didn't see it myself but it's gotta be true they're all like that today even the models haven't you seen
he's building himself a mansion in alphaville
he's living in a mansion in alphaville
and she's struggling to meet the repayments on an apartment in jabaquara
(never wanted to take it to court didn't want to come between him and the boy)
and he needs to get braces
and he learned so much they'd read the weeklies and dailies and discuss all sorts of subjects when he was little he came out with all sorts of questions and now she's the one gobsmacked at an increasingly whacky world and wants to engage with the fight for the environment join greenpeace and that day she came home early tendinitis was the diagnosis and he was taking a shower the computer was on and she went in to pick up the dirty clothes hey ragamuffin and she glances at the screensaver this huge pu— vagina her bag fell to the wooden floor the bunch of keys spilled onto the wooden floor her face so red her heart shrank and she thought of just leaving the

room pretending that nothing but then her son's feet stepped out through the doorway a shocked look his body dripping wet a towel around his waist the ruckus of parakeets in the trees outside the handbag bunch of keys splayed out on the floor the ozzy osbourne poster on the wardrobe door have you eaten son mom he mumbles I and she says I know let's go out to eat, grab a pizza how about it and the night dissipates his schoolmates from the building all jumbled together stoned on weed and paraffin friends she knew parents voices funeral wreathes the chair the headboard the garland of flowers grief he's just a jesuschristy lying there like that a picture bought one sunny sunday at the fair in republica square seventeen in august

so happy so handsome such a companion so well liked so intelligent so loving

my god why why did he go and do it my god why

9. Rats

A rat, on his hind legs, nibbling a crumb, watching his companions as they scuttle across the filth, like characters in a video game. Another, more daring, tries chewing on a rag plastered with gooey poo, still fresh, and, fumbling, it scratches at something soft and warm, which immediately moves, scaring it. Composure regained, it sinks its teeth into the tender flesh, bites down. Excited, the pack descends, convulsing.

The feeble little body, mummified in fetid rags, denounces its discomfort, the leg muscles tense up, the lungs fill, ready to wail, but all that escapes its trembling lips is a galled mewl, a brief spasm. The embarrassed morning light fumbles through the holes in the corrugated roof, through the chinks in the billboard patchwork walls. But inside the shanty it's still night.

The dirty soother the baby was gumming on, with its punctured teat, escaped and rolled onto the sleeping form of his three-year-old sister, sucking her thumb as insatiably as when she used to sup from her mother's breast. She wheezed the whole night, and she coughed and cried, because the flimsy, moth-eaten blanket they'd been given by the Samaritans had been sequestered in a death roll by their brother of six.

The queen-size spring mattress they share came to them one wet afternoon, with dark stains on the torn cloth, nooks spitting dust, roof-racked on a van rattling down the highway in Itapecerica, out of Vila Andrade bound for Jardim Irene, back when they lived with Birôla, a good man, him. He took the kids to the circus once, with clowns, a trained dog in a tutu, monkey on a monocycle, a lion tamer whipping a toothless cat in a cage, parade horses, a trapeze swinger, tightrope walker, sword swallower, toffee apples, girls in leotards, candy floss, magician with a blade box, lollypops, ice cream on a stick. Then he started abusing the eldest, grown up now, but thirteen then. Hacked off, she doused his junk in alcohol, struck a match, and the flames spread through the neighborhood, though she saved her kids. As for the guy, he burned to a crisp in crack-addled sleep, like indigent coal.

The eight-year-old was his, his spitting image, his little man. Last year, or the year before, doesn't matter, he broke out in a rash, all over his back, his belly, his legs, one big sore, the poor thing. Hospitalized, the nurses never heard so much as a squeak from him, not a single moan, a complete angel. She got a telling-off from the doctor, Absurd, he said, Irresponsible, he yelled, he told the social worker to follow the case, the mange of all things, but she never showed up.

They think it's easy, but she's got no strength left, see. Only thirty-five but not a tooth in her head, her bones all rickety, her eyes swollen, skin lusterless, an archipelago of ulcers, head awhirl. Nit eggs hatching in the kinky, vine-mesh hair of the kids and rats breeding in the floorboards, bedbugs and fleas nest down in the sheets and the roaches battle through the crevices. She's asked-begged the thirteen-year-old to help out, but she's a street rat and is never home. She saw her once on Francisco Morato going car to car at the traffic lights scouting for change. She turns up when it gets cold.

The eleven-year-old has a good head on her, she looks after the little-uns. She takes them over to the soup kitchen, takes them for a bath at the Pentecostal church, changes their clothes, takes good care of them, the scallywag. And she puts them to bed too, making up tales full of events and escapades, snatches of stories picked up here or there. And she does it so well: in the dark, the hush of her voice breezes through the fur of the teddy bear shipwrecked in a torrent, it sleepwalks into the tunnel of the ear, incepting dreams even in her mother, moaning softly in a corner, eyes wide under the thrusts of a lean and tattooed body, another she has never seen before.

10. What a woman wants

Pushing her black-rimmed glasses onto the bridge of her nose, the left temple sticky-taped to the hinge, the lenses scratched, the woman strolls into the tiny kitchen and heads for the sink, where, with some difficulty, she releases the tap lever from a noose of wire and elastic bands and washes out a cream-cheese jar, with Sylvester hounding Tweety across a sticker on the side. Her husband, sitting at the table, raises a cup to his lips with his right hand while holding a book open, correctively tilted against a stigmatism, in his left. He takes a start, raises his eyes, *What's got you up?*

Shuffling worn slippers across the floor, the woman approaches the table, picks up a thermos and pours some coffee into her cream-cheese cup, tears a morsel off a loaf of yesterday's bread, which she smothers in margarine, then slides back up against the sink. *What's that you're reading?* she asks, distractedly, her hand coming to rest on the dressing gown she wears over her camisole. He sets the book down on his lap, *The Microphysics of Power . . . Foucault . . . Found it in a secondhand bookstore . . . on João Mendes*, he says, justifying the splurge. The fingers of his left hand shepherd the crumbs on the checkered tablecloth into a unified mound. *Why . . . why are you up so early?*

She opens the louvered window overlooking the street and watches the first passengers waiting in the anemic light for the first bus of the day. She chews the bread and washes it down with a swig of coffee. She turns and lays her eyes on some imaginary X on the far wall, an old teacher's trick, level with the circuit box and midway between the rusty red metal cupboard and the peg-leg yellow refrigerator. *I was coming back from school last night and hit a jam at Limoeiro with a ton of police cars sirens wailing it was chaos and I was alone*

and scared to death I dunno it's like you never know what's going to cross your mind at a time like that
(her husband fills a coffee cup, lights a cigarette, an ant crawls up his open hand).

Then this shootout started and I thought of just running for it but then I figured the car could get robbed imagine that? so I pulled the key from the ignition and lay facedown on the seats I was afraid I was going to die there alone and then something strange happened I must have fainted or something cuz I saw myself a girl again with my friends from the youth club on an outing to who-knows-where and someone was playing guitar and we were singing and laughing and then they started honking behind me and I was startled and started the car and pushed it into first and saw the cops dragging two bodies along the sidewalk by the heels two guys soaked in blood and definitely dead and loads of others sitting on the curb in just their underwear hands behind their heads like something out of an American movie
(the husband uncrosses his legs, stamps his cigarette out on a saucer, glances with affliction at the clock on the wall).

The woman's gaze drifts through the blue plume of smoke slowly wreathing into the glow from the forty-watt bulb.

The neighborhood stretches itself awake

An argument, swiftly aborted
a slamming door
a radio playing
dogs barking
the shutters rolling up on the bakery
quick footsteps on the sidewalk

a shrieking baby
a siren in the distance *"Police?"*

the bus pulls in, the passengers hurry aboard, the bus pulls out
and I decided I don't want to live like this anymore I don't
(the husband is impatient, *"I'm going to be late"*
But . . .
I'm tired nothing's worth the sacrifice we work work work and for what? we hardly ever see each other anymore we never go out and I can't remember the last time you touched me
he lights another cigarette, gets up and walks over to her
It's true . . . it is . . . we have to sit down together and iron some stuff out. . . . But . . . honestly . . . I don't think . . . it's like . . . it's not as bad as all that. . . .
The problem is it never is for you, anything's okay for you.
He tries to wrap his threadbare sea-blue shirt arms around her, but she wriggles free, turns back to the louvered window, where the day is yawning.
I'm overdrawn again at the bank, did you know that? you know why? because we don't earn enough to make ends meet and we can't break the tailspin we're getting in deeper and deeper.
You're shouting. . . .
The German shepherd scratches at the kitchen door, whining anxiously. Against the light, the chiaroscuro of the woman's face.
Keep it down . . . the boys . . . you'll wake the boys. . . . Calm down. . . .

Calm down? I'm tired can't you see? I'm tired tired tired of living with a lunatic who only gives a damn about books that's all books that just clutter the place up and generate fungus that makes the kids sick and all because of a a a lifestyle choice this this option for poverty goddamit what fascinated me ten years ago now just pisses me off

But

Let me speak I'm not finished no let me get this off my chest I never speak

The kids . . . you'll wake them up

I have to hold things together here when you can't even change a lightbulb not even that of course you have many qualities you're faithful honest hardworking but a woman a woman needs more than that much more

But

the problem is I've come to the conclusion a terrible conclusion that deep down you're a you're a conformed nonconformist deep down you just want to go on giving your classes because in the classroom no one pisses you off no one questions you

But

our poverty is a fine excuse for your lack of initiative of boldness of courage you hide your cowardice your lack of vigor behind some intellectual nonconformism as if the world were terrified of your indignation Oooo

But

a woman a woman needs more than that much more my dear you can't see the future love because you don't have one

But

you don't understand you never did you really believe that this is all life is living in a dump mired in debt never having money to buy something different go out for dinner take a trip
But
we just stay stuck in the house tense on our way out tense on our way home praying our kids don't get mixed up with the neighborhood goons or get started on drugs
The husband lights up another smoke, brushes some last crumbs off his clothes, gathers up his books, puts on his glasses,
Sorry I didn't mean to offend you
You didn't . . .
It's just I'm tired
I know. . . . You need a break . . . some rest
No I don't need a . . . oh forget it you wouldn't understand what's the point?
he opens the door, which leads onto a small paved-over yard, a chill breeze rushes in with the dog, tails wagging, the woman draws her gown around her, he caresses her arm,
You have to be strong . . . persistent. . . .
I'm not getting any younger, time is running out
(he pats the German shepherd, awaiting orders, tongue lolling)
Better hose down the yard . . . look at the smell. Down, boy, down!

She locks the door
resting on the door handle
she hears the gate whine
then the engine of the Chevette

barking dogs
footfall on the streets
voices
a revving bus
the creaking gate
the engine of the Chevette
voices

who is this man, my god, this lard-assed, barrel-bellied, friendless man in shabby clothes
who spends his Saturdays washing the dog and sinking beers and sucking snacks off toothpicks in the yard
who spends his Sundays watching football on TV
with cans of beer and snacks on toothpicks
and who sleeps in her bed
and is the father of her children
and who
my god
she just doesn't know anymore
who is this man, who?

11. Massacre nº 41

With a full-on volley, straight to the ribcage, visible beneath the skin, the mongrel was drop-kicked into the middle of the street, where it landed in a heap before scurrying away with a yelp, not yet mindful of the wanton cruelty. Its only urge was to escape down some stinking gully or sleepy alley, through pools of darkness and light, which, mutually encouraged, turned each other inside out. There was no one around now to snatch the newborn day. It stopped, panting, its little heart pounding, as the confused recent memory shuddered through its body. Why had it just been hurt? Rasping, it licks at its coarse, dirt-yellow coat, trying to soothe the pain. Who had it just been hurt by? Its sharp teeth bite blindly at unseen fleas. Exhausted, it lays its head on its outstretched paws, closes its eyes and sighs, as its tail stops wagging. The colored shards slowly settle down the back of the kaleidoscope. It had gone peeking through the drapes of night in search of its owner, ears piqued and at the ready, as it knew all about Vila Clara, having been driven out before, booted out, chased away by buckets of scalding water, hurled rocks, bangers, fireworks, cudgels, bullets even, yes sir, even bullets! when, near the dance hall where jigging feet kicked up puffs of cement dust, it had spied an intriguing scene: beneath a lamppost, as if sleeping, three bodies lay in a heap. It crept cautiously closer, to investigate further. Drunks these weren't, he knew that, he had experience. Patient, he had long accompanied the stations of his master's cross like a canine Magdalena, watching him liquidate himself in dive bar after dive bar, getting tangled up in trees, his spine curved over a sack of recyclable cans. But these, these reeked of sweat soured by the bittersweet zing of fear. Pellets of lead had ricocheted off the outer walls of the car mechanic's workshop, gouging lumps out of a giant spray-painted Ayrton Senna—later, the ballistics people would collect twenty-three 38-caliber bullet cases. Blood had spilled from numerous perforations in the skin, gathering in crimson-red pools that spread across the sidewalk, trickled over the curb and curled into two rivulets that barely licked the asphalt before beginning the slow seep into the earth. He concentrated and tried to recognize the faces, two of the three were mere boys, and then he felt the sharp pang just above the lung and nearly retched what little he'd had to eat. He tucked in his tail, pulled back his ears, and bolted, disappearing into the dark. His eyes widened with fright, the noises that come with the sun had started to rise, his right hind-leg paw scratched his cankerous ear, he had to find his owner, who liked to talk to him, pet his balding body, kiss his snout, play tickles, use him as a pillow, who shared his leftovers with him. A few days ago, in the afternoon, he'd stretched out on the grassy island on the avenue, and that was the last he'd seen of him. All that was left was the sack of flattened cans.

12. Taurus

The new moon in the house of Cancer calls for retreat and reflection. After the agitation of the last few days, it's time for a slower, more continuous pace. Those who lose the run of themselves may regret it later. Radical attitudes are to be avoided and condemned. The cluster of planets in Taurus, earthy and possessive, tends to trigger excess, but the lunar energy is soothing.

13. Still life

The teacher turned the key in the lock and pushed the door. *Eh!* something was blocking the way, how strange. She put her shoulder into it and it finally gave way, a slow flood tide tumbling wreckage in its drag. *What the . . . ?* The scrum of kids at her back peeked inside, startled but curious. Through the chink in the door, weak morning light fell across the bulletin board—green felt on plywood—jarred between the baseboard and the door handle, the doodles and drawings still stuck on with tacks.

The corridor that led into the three classrooms was littered with crushed chalk, trails of colored glue, cakes of modeling clay, and stomped-on sheets of paper. A blackboard lay on the vomit-stained floor, alongside torn-up projects and paintbrushes daubed in feces that had been used to leave arabesques and illegible scrawls on the white walls. There was a Coca-Cola can full of piss, and a makeshift crack pipe—a biro barrel stuck sideways into a Yakult bottle. Down the back, a broken lock, shattered glass, shards of a clay water filter, boot dents in the side of the stove, bashed-up pots and pans. In the rush, shouts and cries rebounded off the French roof tiles, as eyes roamed in search of explanations.

She was pulled by the elbow, amid whining voices, "The vegetable garden, the vegetable garden . . . ," the kids marched her out into the yard: before her were furrows of trashed vegetables: carrot shoots, beetroot, lettuces, cauliflower, tomatoes, all plucked and strewn, so much loving care wasted, none of it would grow back. The kids trod carefully among the tiny green cadavers, eyes heavy, and she, staring out across the sprawl, observed the scandalous bare brick houses, skeletal columns, concrete platforms, kites afloat in the gray sky, the stench of sewers, a twitch in her left eyelid, solitude and despair.

14. An Indian

Old Aprígio would be the one to best recall the day the Indian first turned up round here, but he passed away yesterday, riddled with throat cancer, and they always say it's down to liquor and cigarettes, but I don't believe that, he never drank a day in his life, except sodas; as for tobacco, well he couldn't even stand the smell of smoke, the Lord take him! All anyone knows is that the sav rolled into the bar one afternoon, laid his bald potbelly on the greasy red Formica counter, and ordered a shot in that weird language of his, someone found it funny and spotted him a shot, and the coot knocked them back all night, getting more and more pissed, then he goes into the middle of the road and starts to dance, and the rednecks all huddle round him in a circle, clapping, and the coot gets carried away and starts stripping off to rampant applause till his junk's all hanging out, in front of the kids and women in the street. Well, between the wasters and the workers, mayhem took over that corner of town, until someone, there's always a spoilsport, called the cops. They sent in the heavy hitters, who arrived, sirens wailing, tires screeching, and they spilled out of the car and started dishing it out left right and center, and the hillbillies beat it, quick as a flash, while the calm-down brigade tried to explain that the guy was an Indian, like a real Indian, not like the other deadbeats, who were just deadbeats, so the fact that his bits were out, but they weren't having none of it, waving their batons about, and the sav was just stood there, buck naked, swoon-drunk, totally out of it. Grabbed, cuffed, dragged, they slung him in the drunk tank. Sometime later he turned up again, wearing a beat-up flowery synthetic-satin shirt and threadbare jeans, flip-flops on his feet and that same dumbass grin. He came into old Aprígio's bar, at the last stop on the 6068 line (Jardim Varginha–Santo Amaro), laid his bald potbelly on the greasy red Formica counter and said in that weird language of his that he wanted something to eat. Old Aprígio says to him, *If you want to eat you have to pay*, and the Indian beamed at him with that dumbass grin, either not understanding or pretending not to, cuz you never can tell with his kind, whether they're being sincere or they're playing you. Aprígio tried to explain, *Go earn some money! Tutu! Dosh! Dinheiro! Moola! See!* and he rubbed the tip of his forefinger against his thumb, but the sav just stared, flashing his perfect teeth. Aprígio gave up, skewered a slice of sausage, and handed it to him. He wolfed it down and pointed at the greasy tray, asking for more. So Aprígio looks at him and says, *Ah yeah? So you're gonna have to work for it,* and he snatches a mop, a squeegee, a bucket of soapy water, and a tin of creolin. *Here, go wash the stalls,* and the fool looks at him and says yes, *Then the floor . . . and all this dirt*, and the fool stands there, smiley eyes wide. So Aprígio pulls open the restroom door, and out wafts the pissy reek, and he splashes out some of the soapy water and starts mopping hard, *See?* and he hands it to the apprentice, *Now you*, and the fool says yes, but doesn't move. So Aprígio shoves the mop into his hand and starts repeating the movements, *Like this, see?* and the sav starts mopping, all awkward, and Aprígio says, *That's it, Indy, you're getting the hang of it! Now the squeegee, right, yeah . . . good . . . that's it . . .* Out in the bar, the Indian fell to spirited work, handling mop and squeegee with aplomb, *That's it, Indy, looking good!* On his haunches in the doorway, the Indian devoured a salami sandwich, licked his fingers and asked for more, then a whole boiled egg, three pork rinds, a chicken dumpling, two kibbes, a rissole, a pastry, all widows from the counter display, and then some corn cake on top, a bottomless pit. *Off with you now. Move it on!* and old Aprígio sent him on his way, pulled down the shutters, and headed upstairs. Night had fallen heavy on the street outside, and old Aprígio took a look out the window and saw the sav stretched out on the pavement in front of the doorway, like a guard dog, and he thought, *Least no one's gonna be breaking in tonight. . . .* When he woke up every morning there was the Indian. He'd fold up the shutters and the sav would fetch the bucket, the mop, the squeegee, the box of soap, the creolin and he'd mop out the restroom, the barroom, wash the pile of glasses in the sink, hose down the sidewalk, and wash old Aprígio's orange Beetle. He was known like the begging-ass, as far out as the settlements in Olinda, Auri-Verde, Jardim Alcântara II, and even Jardim Marilda: he cleared plots, babysat, ran messages, carried shopping bags, swept down paving slabs, the kids ragging him nonstop. Wednesdays and Saturdays he feasted on the feijoada stew, his favorite dish. At Sunday barbecues, he spent the day sinking beers and grilling chicken wings. Some of us reckoned he was Guarani from Parelheiros, the Curucutu village; others said he was Pankararu, from the shanty at Real Parque, in Morumbi; but most said he'd hitched all the way down from the Amazon or Mato Grosso, and was dumped there, maybe just for the fun of it, who knew? And the subject always came up again when we were done talking sports and women. The half-wit disappeared every now and then, without a word, and we'd speculate: some would say he'd gone to visit family in the forest; others, that he was in the drunk tank again. The truth was, we never knew for sure. Even when the cancer silenced old Aprígio, sucked away the meat and the muscle and the marrow in his bones, and nothing helped, neither radio nor chemo, and the doctors decided that morphine was the only thing for it, and he was holed up in a ward, the Indian was nowhere to be found. When they let him home to die last week, the sav finally reappeared. He slept in the bar doorway, two whole days, with nothing to eat or drink, silent as the dying man himself. Yesterday, after he learned of Aprígio's passing, he went wandering, shriveled and alone, in the miserable streets of Jardim Varginha, a bottle of hooch under his arm. Some folks say they've seen him stumbling about in the harsh night, but then this morning I found him stretched out under the tarpaulin of a hardware store on Santo Amaro Avenue, hugging an empty bottle, out of it, oblivious to everything, everything.

15. Fran

Yes, she'd promised not to drink, Françoise recalls as she grabs the bottle by the neck, but just one drop, just a single drop of liquor tipped into the oily surface of her morning coffee, just to stay the shakes?

She looks at herself in the crystal mirror, a window that catches snatches of the sitting room and the lead streak of the polluted morning. Shrieking parakeets. Having just woken up, her skin, au naturel, reveals a hint of wrinkles, few in fact, just laughter-lines really, the crow's-feet of stress, maybe. She opens her dressing gown and her shapely breasts roll out, attractive, still pert, still scalpel virgins. Her hand slides down to her belly, any fat? any stretch marks? cellulite? She pouts with pride: *Hot!* She turns, checks her behind, her freckled back, pert butt, dangerous thighs: *Hot!*

At the tiny table, she scrapes out the last remnants of strawberry jam from a jar and spreads it onto the bumpy surface of a cream cracker with the tip of the blade. She lifts it to her mouth. She flings away the cracker and the knife, sends the empty jar rolling across the carpet, unbroken. *Shit! Shit! Shit!* She gets up and rushes out onto the balcony. Blue tears threaten to ruin her day *Calm down, Fran, easy!* trickling down her throat. *Easy now, easy. The phone will ring, Fran, soon, soon. And you'll need to be clearheaded. Clearheaded! Just imagine, Hello, yes this is Fran, crash! You hit the floor like a . . . like a mango . . . a ripe mango. . . .*

The wind stirs the smell, from the mango-strewn yard below, ripe mangoes, ubá mango, Madame Françique, Valencia pride, dappled mangoes, pigs eating mangoes, birds eating mangoes, ducks, chickens, horses, oxen eating mangoes, interweaving patches of cold, humid shade, overlapping, an orgy of foliage and branches and erstwhile roots from a long-gone field on a lea rim, in an empty grotto in the backlands of Rio state, on the world's fringe, and she chews on the jamless cracker, *Better that way, keep my figure*, she sips from the steaming coffee.

In the past she worked for Globo TV, doing supporting roles, cameos, walk-on appearances on Sunday variety shows, sometimes the villain, sometimes the foil. She was even being stopped in the street at one point, prodded, tugged at, touched up, Aren't you on TV? *TV . . . TV is not for just anyone, only a select few.* She never fell into the graces of the right director, the right actor, the right producer, the right agent. *Patience. No whoring it.* Theater, just serious stuff. *But none came up? Patience.* Cinema, it'll come. But no porn, neither soft- nor hard-core. Pose nude in a men's mag? she was open to proposals. But only tasteful poses, no gynecological stuff.

Was that the phone? *Fran? Augusto, Augusto Bicalho, how are things? Listen, I've got just the right part for you, it's a—.* No, the phone didn't ring. She dips an unpainted finger in her whiskey and sucks on it. Fran knows how to wait. During her regression therapy, rooting through her past lives, she encountered her karma: in a click of her fingers, the desert sands bowed before the selfish princess. She is paying now, in this incarnation, the price of that arrogance. Numerology helped her rewrite her name, Frannçoise (with two *n*'s) Pernaud, more energy, more shine. And those lumbar pains she'd had since childhood, she got rid of those with a combination of Reiki massage and meditation.

Lounging on the sofa, she sips a second shot of whiskey, straight, then checks the phone volume, *The sound is on, maximum*, she had to hand back her cell phone because she couldn't afford the bills, she picks up the receiver, *yes, the line's good.* She leafs through *The Seven Spiritual Laws of Success*, Deepak Chopra, and the letters rebel, the lines tremble, her Japanese neighbor is Opus Dei, they slipped his mail under her door by mistake, and she opened it, curious, but she can't remember now what it was all about, she tore it up, burned it in the toilet bowl, flushed it down. She sometimes bumps into the Japanese woman in the elevator, says good morning, with her two Pokémons in tow, they're an overprotected bunch, so much so they spend their lives looking for a surrogate mother. . . . *Geishas . . . Horny devils . . .*

A year in this tiny apartment already, in Jardim Jussara, when asked, she says she lives in Morumbi, which is not entirely a lie, as you can see Francisco Morato Avenue from the window, where kids go car to car at traffic lights asking for change, she lies down on the sofa, takes a third swig of whiskey, straight, checks the volume on the phone, *Maximum, okay,* picks up the phone, checks the line, *yes, it's working,* Ah Augusto, good-old Augusto, her calls always go straight to his voice mail, **Leave a message after the**, at the agency, Miriam's mantra, **Sure, leave it with me, dear, I'll have him call you as soon as he gets back, I'm sure he knows what it's about, rest assured**

16. Like this

swimming pools like little blue lakes (stork nests built in the chimneys of) the laptop, the fingers of his right hand pick at the knot (**the two of us, galeria vittorio emmanuele, milan, remember?**) the gray bar of the horizon (putrid, the air) *seen from a height sao paulo isn't all that*
—the day will come when we won't even be able to leave the house
—but aren't we already living in fortresses? *The violence*
(Johannesburg, you know it? *ugly so filthy and so*
You can't go out at night) *dangerous*
government come government go, what changes? When it comes to looking for campaign donations they're all sweetness and light. But the recompense . . . tiny racetrack (:jailbait that girl—show me let me see

I won't tell any) propellers over the river (putrid, the water) (**I know, I hate scandal too, but you**)
—I'm not insensitive to the social angle *unrecognizable, downtown rife with peddlers, pickpockets, human placards, stench of urine stench of saturated fats stench of* he runs his hand through his thinning hair (**my mother used to don gloves, hat, and high heels to take a stroll on the Chá Viaduct, me, as a boy, very young, I used to run on the**) this is the country of the future? god is brazilian? where there was a riverhead yesterday there's a shantytown today where there was a school yesterday now there's a prison where yesterday there was a turn-of-the-century mansion house now it's all three-suite apartments, two hundred square feet apiece
—a jeep lengthwise across the road ferreira braked the bodyguards came up behind, guns blazing, ferreira backed up and we escaped down the wrong side of the road I spent a whole week popping *they're all immigrants from bahia minas all northeastern vagrants with no love for the city so they don't give a* (**you and your four hundred years can go and**) what they made was a magnificent city those minarets (putrid, the city)
—the youngest is in paris, took a doctorate in architecture
—the middle one is here, works in the purchasing department you know the gutter of any company
—the eldest is with our partners in new york
The minister says he will definitely sign the decree it's all ready (**you and yours**) the morning breeze soothes paulista avenue the heliport swells atop the (putrid, this country) *we're going to have to reinvent civilization*

17. The wait

Startled, eyes flap open, sun, ten fifteen on the alarm clock, bedspread in a heap on the floor, pillow in a leg-lock, strands of his long hair hide his face, he sits on the edge of the bed, stretches, gets up, a draft hits him through the half-open louvers, the red roof tiles of Vila Santo Stéfano, Imigrantes expressway in the distance.

Shirtless, gray gym slacks, his Raider sandals shuffle across the linoleum to the kitchen. Perched on the burner of the gas stove, a stuffed coffee filter lolls in a dark green pot with little white flowers along the side. The foam of heated milk still clings to the black Tefal, a lid sits ungainly on a pressure cooker containing the leftovers of some chicken soup. On the refrigerator door, stuck on with magnets (an avocado, a chayote, and an ad for a drugstore), he finds a note:

Don't be late now, son
I'll be rooting for you
Good luck
Kisses
Mom

He crumples the note and throws it into a small bin overflowing with banana skins on the wet drainboard. He grabs two slices of bread, plasters them with margarine, slaps them into a stove toaster, lights the ring, then pours some milk into the pot and lights another ring. He yawns and waits, with a cigarette in his mouth and an old comic in his hand. He takes out the toast and bungles the charred slices onto the tablecloth, wiggling his burnt fingertips. He picks up the thermos flask half full of cold coffee and spills some into the warm milk. Still standing, he chomps the toast, fidgets with the comic, the cigarette, as the breeze stirs through the hair on his arms and his bare chest, he chews and swallows, slurps the milky coffee, wipes his hands on his gray gym pants.

He pushes a footstool into a corner and reaches up to where there's a gap between the wall tiles and the coving, and pulls out a small plastic parcel. He unwraps the stick of marijuana, crumbles off a corner into a rollie paper, then slides the stash back into the hole. His gray sweatpants drag and his Raider sandals shuffle back across the red linoleum into his room, where he turns on the stereo—"Hallowed Be Thy Name," Iron Maiden—at full volume, lights the joint, sucks in the smoke, lies back, eyes closed, and sucks in the smoke. Then he sprays some air freshener and throws open the balcony windows, revealing an array of lonely domestic vignettes outside.

With a black elastic band strangling his hair into a ponytail, he strolls off down Sérgio Cardoso Street wearing a black Helloween T-shirt, baggy pants of undeterminable color, filthy Reeboks, and a pendant dangling from his right earlobe. He stops off at a convenience store to buy some cigarettes and a pocket lighter, then rides the bus to Saúde subway station, switching lines at Sé, bound for República Square. Emerging from the mouth of the escalator, the Itália Building looms large behind him, and he wades into a roar of cars and trucks fried prawn balls chicken dumplings kibbes pastels, voices block-and-tackle, blend, annihilate each other at newsstands, over newspapers, used books, earrings, collars, wristbands, chokers, rings, woolen tunics, ponchos, blouses, shawls, packed bus stops, pickpockets, shoe shiners, popcorn carts, homemade desserts, vagrants, bowled-over crawling drunks, bums, junkies, cripples.

The interview's at 2 p.m., corner of Ipiranga and Consolação, *There's time*, so he browses the store at the Rock Gallery, *some wicked stuff*, a temptation, but not a cent in his pocket, except the bus fare home, a bummer, so he spills back out, Conselheiro Xavier de Toledo, Braúlio Gomes, Dom José Gaspar Square, São Luis and Ipiranga Avenues. At a wall across the street, he idly smokes and surveys the entrance to the building: a weigh-a-plate buffet on the ground floor; three steps up, yellowed marble, the corners broken off; and up there, on the seventh floor, in some sauna-hot hellhole with plywood partitions, enigmatically ensconced behind a file-strewn desk, with a gray filing cabinet at his back and a few arcane accountancy books on top, some suit sits there waiting to conduct what will be his tenth interview in two months, his *tenth interview*!

(That night, his alarmed mother, leaning against the doorjamb, pressure cooker in hand, watches the news on the box, as the colors splay and stain the sitting-room walls, her son went out looking for work and has not come home, nor has he called, *my god, has something happened to him?* When the ads come on, she swishes back into the kitchen, where she starts to reheat yesterday's chicken soup.)

18. List

Announcer/Animator

Galvanizer

Gardener
Governess
Installer—telephones
Installer—telephone lines
Installer—sound systems
Instructor—training
Instrumentalist—electronic
Instrumentalist—mechanical
Laminator
Manager—administrative
Manager—administrative industrial
Manager—data-processing center
Manager—deli
Manager—industrial
Manager—marketing
Manager—operations
Manager—shop
Motor boater
Oil technician—automotive
Oil technician—industrial
Plasterer
Printer—flexographic
Printer—general
Printer—offset
Printer—offset (Davidson)
Printer—offsetting machine
Printer—typographic
Printer—silkscreen
Quality inspector

SECURITY GUARD

SECURITY GUARD—female

SUPERVISOR—cleaning and gardening

WAITER

WASHER—automobiles

WASHER—vehicles

WASHER—windows

WELDER—(Ah!)

WELDER—primary to junior high, 2 years' experience, aged 28 to 50

WELDER—no educational requirements, 12 months' experience, aged 25 to 45

19. Brabeza

Four afternoons left to Mother's Day and not a dime in his pocket. He'd picked out a radio-cassette recorder, AM/FM, she'd love that, being hooked on the ads and all, with nothing better to do I guess. . . . Ideal, of course, would be a twenty-inch Toshiba with built-in VCR. He'd clocked up hours casing the window display at Extra-Mappin in Ramos Square, checking the prices, installments, hmmm, that's complicated! proof of employment, proof of address, social security number, two references, hmmm, impediments! No, he'd have to find some other way, another radio, after all, the old lady, she wasn't picky, not even expecting nothing anyway, so whatever she got would be a bonus, a surprise to tickle her pink. To work, then! An AM/FM, radio-cassette recorder and Bob's your uncle. Now: where to find the cash? Brabeza loiters. The best place to pick pockets is Barão de

Itapetininga, where there are ATMs. People grab their wads, stuff them into wallets or handbags, then scurry off, all wary. Women are better: you spot one and tail her, the time always comes when they let their guard down, then you snatch the bag or slice the leather (leather my ass!), pluck the dough, and slink off whistling. If she's got a cell phone, then all the better. Depending on the day, three hits should cover the radio-cassette recorder with enough left over for a Big Mac at the McDonald's on Henrique Schaumann, where it tastes better. Men are harder targets. Skinny and pug-ugly, Brabeza is easy prey if the mule decides to fight back, lay on some knuckles, then it's bye-bye, game over! So he stakes out the Bradesco ATM, watching from a safe distance, camouflaged by the bustle and the crowd. There's also the fact that he's still green and ashamed of thieving, keeps on remembering his mother, who'd be mortified if she knew, sweet Jesus! might even die of shame. So no gang stuff: just himself, on his downtown stage. He's not the ambitious type, so as soon as he straightens things out he'll go legit, conscience clear. But in the meantime, he can't leave his mom in the lurch, bed-ridden like this, with some unidentified disease. He has to give her a bath, change her clothes, help her take a dump, a pee, it's a mess. He was busted once, though he'd nothing on him, having returned to the gutter's teeth the (genuine) leather wallet, gravid with cash and documents. At the precinct, after the customary kicking, the lady couldn't ID him, so he started hollering about his honest search for work, his employment stamps (all false)—"I'm not a thief, me; I'm no thief!" he whimpers. So the woman gets all indignant and starts decrying the injustice being done, then hands him her business card—lawyer—and says he should call her, they'd sue the state for . . . get this . . . torture! Absurd, torture! Oh yeah, and she'll let him know if any work comes up, then she turns around and is gone. Brabeza crumpled up her card and returned it to the garbage bin, was she crazy? put himself in their hands and he'd never be able to work in peace again. He slipped into a secondhand bookstore on Riachuelo, and his legs almost went from under him, surrounded by all that booky silence, he only didn't faint because God winked at him, sparing him the humiliation. The simple truth was he took no pleasure at all from thieving. Maybe if he tanked up before, like the bank robbers and express kidnappers, but drugs? Not for him; he'd smoked a joint once and it sent his heart pounding so fast he thought he was going to die, then he bombed out green on a bench in Roosevelt Square, woke up a zombie and rode the first bus home to mama and her apron strings. On the way he tried to make up some excuse, but when it came to it he just blurted some crap about spending the night with a girl, that's my boy? like hell, and he took one on the ear, "Listen here, boy," another clip round the ear, "You'll end up getting the girl in the family way. Just you wait and see! Then she'll pack me off to a home. . . . Is that what you want, fool? See the back of your ole momma? Imbecile!" So he'd try not to be late so momma wouldn't think he was getting frisky with the inexistent hussy. So that was that, then; downtown it was: Largo da Concórdia to Luz Terminal; República Square to Dom Pedro Park. In with the peddlers, the security guards, the cops, the bums, taking it nice and easy, lying in wait on Barão de Itapetininga, scanning the crowd to see who was going to foot the bill for an AM/FM radio-cassette recorder for Mrs. Chiquinha.

20. We could have been such good friends

We could have been such good friends.

I'd invite him over for dinner on Saturday night, at our place, and we'd serve up a whopping leg of New Zealand lamb garnished with rosemary and accompanied by an honest red from Bacalhôa, and we'd listen—raptured—to the latest Chico Buarque, *The Best of Dinah Washington*, and another singer whose name escapes me, but whose album I bought at Tower Records in London.

We'd be introduced to his wife, already briefly spied at the pool, and after a couple of glasses we'd leave the Spanish velvet sofa for the rough thatch of the chairs in the kitchen—somewhat smaller than we'd wish—where we'd help Célia, wrapped in an apron with surrealist motifs down the front, with the roast and the salad, chicory sprinkled with sesame seeds, beds prepared for slabs of smoked salmon. I'd wash the dishes while he and his wife cleared the table, tablecloth, cutlery, glasses, table mats. After dinner, restored to the comfort of the sitting room, we'd lose ourselves in the ebb and flow of conversation and, as the night wore on, when we no longer had the energy even to change the CD, when the street outside was already empty of cars, there'd be a touch of guilt, burnished by alcohol, about having left the kids with friends or relatives for the night, then we'd finish off our last topic and say goodnight, promising this would be the first of many such evenings.

Our friendship would consolidate with time. I'd confide in him about an affair I've been having with a girl from work, the director's assistant, who, though not exactly beautiful, has a great body and, more's the point, believes every word I say, and then I'd reveal that my left incisor is an implant, because I lost it in a car crash on the way back from a long weekend at a farm hotel in Serra Negra, and that I miss my mother like hell, dead ten years now, and how she used to brush my hair even after I was grown up, and that Célia and I have been having problems, even thinking about divorce, but then there's Joana, five, and Afonsinho, seven, and that it's proven fact that kids from broken homes have a harder time of it when they hit their teens, and we'd never forgive ourselves if, heaven forbid, someday, one of them should, you know, so we try to handle conflicts as they arise.

I'd tell him all of that. And I'd also arrange for us to go halves on renting a beach house in Barra do Sahy, where a Saturday and Sunday of sun and surf would do us the world of good, we'd take the Imigrantes highway together, our Vectra and his Golf overtaking each other until we run into the mother of all traffic jams, but even the holdup adds to the fun, what with the kids wanting to switch cars, with the boys in one and the girls in the other. The wives would gab on and on about housemaids, breast implants, Botox, and lipo to suck away spare tires, but we'd know that such dreams don't come true because, besides being really expensive, the health plans don't cover cosmetic surgery. Then we'd point to our beer bellies, his premature baldness, my graying hair, and they'd say, Yeah, see? You guys have it easy even with that, because women like the older man, with more experience, and we'd say, No way, that's all in the past, today women want their toy-boys, and with this the traffic jam would have unraveled and off we'd go, okay, see you down on the coast!

We'd exchange e-mail addresses and fill up one another's in-boxes with spam, Portuguese jokes, chain mail, online petitions, warnings about the latest viruses, the most recent innovations in street crime, some racy pics, porn, cartoons, and even some interesting tips on websites, virtual CD and book stores, and we'd discover affinities we never knew we had, and every Friday we'd meet for happy hour at a bar in Lapa where they serve "the best aperitifs in São Paulo," and we'd sit there assessing the hotness of every chick within range of our telescopic vision and dis the mayor, the governor, the president of the republic, and reveal to each other that our current accounts are in the red, that the kids' schools aren't as good as we'd been led to believe, that it's becoming harder and harder to keep on fucking the wife and that we've been buying *Playboy* on the sly, and then we'd confess that we've been lying to our pals about our extramarital flings and that we haven't really been doing anyone "on the side," and I'd tell him that the director's assistant does exist, but that the only time I ever spoke to her was to apologize for knocking her ice cream onto the canteen floor, and after all that we'd roll home, reeling from the alcohol, and the wives would go all ninja about us being nothing but "skirt chasers," saying that "men are all the same," and then we'd end the night in a god-awful funk after the mother of all domestics, but grateful nonetheless because it means we don't have to lie there trying to get horny, and in the morning, Saturday, we'd wake up early and go buy fish and vegetables at the fair.

But, the fact is, we don't know each other at all. I've bumped into him a couple of times in the elevator, on the way to our cars in the parking lot or out by the pool, with him reading a weekly and me swimming with Joana and Afonsinho.

But I found out today that he won't be coming home.

He was caught in one of those express kidnappings.

Seems they grabbed him on República do Líbano Avenue, stole his documents, his checkbook, credit and debit cards.

Later, on some wasteland near the Guarapiranga reservoir, they made him kneel in the scrub and put a bullet in the back of his head.

The body was found there this morning.

Still no sign of the car.

21. him)

The day was kinda like this, pure botheration, no place good, just this roaming tingling in his hands, arms, legs, pure disinterest in everything, no will to talk, desire to dig himself a hole and lock himself away in there: **Corinthians are playing tonight. . . . Aren't you going?** a windy head, windblown thoughts, his body aches, rain on the skyline, he types, what's that? tables, he stops, reads it back, hmm . . . double Dutch, the sun must be shining outside, the streets abustle, vehicles honking, fumes spewing, noise, and the tenth floor a doldrums, with wonky air-conditioning—too hot with a pullover, too cold without one—his body whines, shrinks into a cave, shrouded head to toe with a twill of sweat, air! air! he gets up, stretches, goes mix with his species down on Faria Lima Avenue, walk,

walk, entrenched behind a seatback on the bus, Paulistana, PI, a name, some initials, blotting on his ID card, a name, some initials, nothing, not a single memory, of the drought his father the silence, Piauí is my fluey body, rests his forehead against the gun barrel the thief's manic startled eyes, but thin fingers rattle on the keyboard, suits affidavits addenda minutes memos terms of agreement considerations litigation cases pendencies citations summonses aggravations mitigations appeals notifications interpellations

but,

what's the day like? lovely? nasty!

hot? chilly?

has the wind blown away the clouds or are they dousing the asphalt with gentle rain?

a motorcycle courier is lying splat on the crosswalk?

an executive just bitchslapped a streetkid with his laptop?

a bus conductor has intervened to stop a robbery?

and the world, has it ended?

At eight o'clock, inside the tint-glass box, he switches on his PC, sits at the crammed pine desk, lunchtime, devours a burger from the deli on the corner, if he could he'd eat at his desk, but the boss *It ruins the keyboards. . . . It's the crumbs, see . . . they get in between the keys and jam the whole thing up, it's crap! And, shit, if you spill some coke then it's fucked altogether!* napkins soak up the spillage on the Formica top between the restrooms, the oil-slick burger with mustard ketchup mayo, he takes a whiz, brushes his teeth (careful with the steel-wire straitjacket), stows his toiletries, checks himself in the mirror, he wishes he could just kick it all to ——, but there's his IT tuition fees, the installments on his braces, the Mother's Day gift, the CD he's promised his little sister, so his fingers do some acrobatics and it's back to the asdfghjklç, with a yawn, before someone comes along to bust his

22. (her

So light in her sweet sixteens, surgically whitened her sneakers glide millimeters over the cobblestones that pave Direita Street. She sighs. On the ground, she dodges canvas and black sacks, tarpaulin stretched over stalls which her eyes peruse, jeans, Chinese knockoffs, medicinal herbs, bootleg tapes, pirate CDs, fruit stalls, perfumery from Paraguay, chameleonic knickknacks: hawk and peddle. A fat mist sits in this canyon. Music, tunes, they spill, they squawk, they billow (up there on the seam of the sky, with stuck-on building tops, is a brown-gray farm) toward the gray, the gas and diesel fumes gobbed by buses grumbling at the curb in Sé and Patriarca Squares. Her thighs power her along the Chá Viaduct. At the newsstand in front of the Municipal Theater there's a display of rings, dozens of them, which she examines with no attention at all, Ah! the red stone on her ring finger, hmm . . . which sort of resembles an *S*, **Beautiful, ain't it, love?** she hands it back, **Ah! Buy it, love?** she smiles, intimidated, in her surgically whitened sneakers, **Go on . . . take it, I'll give you a discount**. . . . O my heart, Ui! walk away, temptation's setting glue, walk away, legs in motion, each in its sleeve of dark blue uniform, and she strides through the do-re-mis from the crackling loudspeakers by some peddler's stall, the fa-so-la-tis pounding from the loudspeakers outside the department stores, the claves that the tattooed busker cranks from some folksy instrument, and the do-re-mi-fa-so-la-tis mingling at the junction of Conselheiro Crispiniano and Vinte e Quatro de Maio, hunger stirs, motorcycles long queues crutches, buses, files of pedestrians on Largo do Paissandú, she thinks of stopping to eat, what's she got in her purse? enough for a weigh-a-plate? Red light, she crosses the street, driving the shadows before her, Ah! just someone decent, that's all, the religious kind, have kids, a home, away from the gangland shithole she's in today, with the dead askew on the asphalt on Monday, rapes on Saturday, robberies Tuesday, Wednesday, forget the excited sweat of the steam engine chugging at her ass, cupping her breasts, at Shopping Light, never asking the price, Madam, all the shoeboxes off the shelf, Madame, **Hey, love . . . how about doing a portfolio? Gorgeous . . . ! Hey, here's my card. . . .** Oldest trick in the book! Fernanda, the fool, fell for it hook line and even did some nude shots, For *Playboy*, for Globo, like hell! never did see him again, must have sold the pics, no shortage of sleazebags out there, skinmags hanging from strings on every sidewalk. Standing, kebab in hand, wrapped in a napkin, she chews and sips the free juice from a red plastic cup, slowly, whiling away the minutes before it's time to head back to Direita Street.

23. If the customers had arrived

with a plastic yellow bucket full of soapy-blue water and a plastic yellow mop in hand, the two cleaners scrub down the cracked cement sidewalk, slushing the red liquid into the gutter, a foamy rivulet trickles into the grid just as the first customers of the day pull up outside the restaurant and hand the car keys to the valet who smiles through goodafternoons, afternoon, what happened here? Nothing, sir, a little problem, but it's all sorted now

. . . if the customers had arrived just ten minutes earlier they'd have seen the two corpses one with its face smashed in on the curb, a now useless leg bent up over the back like some ungainly pelican the other like a coal sack hurriedly stuffed full of bones or a crushed alarm clock with a wheel here, a spring there

. . . if the customers had arrived just a half an hour earlier they'd have seen the spectacle of two workmen up on a rotten wooden platform suspended from a high-rise by thin ropes washing the gleaming windows one by one, the glass reflecting the two workmen and the platform making four workmen and two platforms one imitating the other BusterKeatonly larking around priding themselves on a job well done, windows men and women will soon stare out of, watching the city, but never from the view they've got never from the angle they now behold of the street below and the surrounding area with its many roofs and they consider themselves lucky chaps indeed to be able to savor the luxury of such a view with the clouds gliding across the glass front and the wind caressing their sunkissed faces and they scoff at the unemployed down there green with envy for not having jobs
and at the employed down there green with envy for not having that job
aboard a sailboat on a glistening fresh-fruit morning ocean

. . . if the couple now savoring a glass of tapada do chaves over furtive glances as her left hand succumbs to the reaching fingers of his right had arrived six and a half hours earlier to see the two workmen clock on, one coming off a bus-subway-bus from ponte rasa and the other off two buses-train-subway from osasco, they'd have heard tomorrow's payday what's your reckoning for the corinthians game I'll put a beer on that ah but I've got to pick up something for the kids to give their mom for Mother's Day on Sunday

24. A bookshelf

HITLER—Joachim Fest
BASIC MARKETING—Marcos Cobra
THE RED AND THE BLACK—Stendhal
ON LIFE AND DEATH—Hans Killian
THE ADVENTURES OF SHERLOCK HOLMES—Conan Doyle
THE VALKYRIES—Paulo Coelho
BRAZIL THE FRUSTRATED SUPERPOWER—Limeira Tejo
TERESA BATISTA HOME FROM THE WARS—Jorge Amado
WAR MOON—Tom Cooper
THEATER 1—Maria Clara Machado
WOMEN IN LOVE—D. H. Lawrence
BRAZILIAN SOCIAL AND POLITICAL
ORGANIZATION—Professor Hermógenes
THE JAPANESE PALACE—José Mauro de Vasconcelos
THE CLOWNS OF GOD—Morris West
VARIOUS TALES—Monteiro Lobato
THE CLOWN—Alexandre Herculano

Exiles of the Chapel—Edgard Armond
Helping Yourself with Self-Hypnosis—Frank S. Caprio
The Iron Chancellor—J. L. Rochester
What Your Hand Reveals—Jo Sheridan
The Greatest Salesman in the World—Og Mandino
The Magic Lantern: An Autobiography—
Ingmar Bergman
Gabriela Clove and Cinnamon—Jorge Amado
Memoirs of a Mangy Lover—Groucho Marx
Marketing Management—John A. Howard
The Gestapo—Sven Hassel
The Moneychangers—Arthur Hailey
The Bhagavad Gita—A. C. Bhaktivedanta
Swami Prabhupada
Secret Formula—Rick Allen
Dry Lives—Graciliano Ramos
Himmler—Alan Wykes
Illusions—Richard Bach
Reunion—Carlos Drummond de Andrade
Dogs of War—Frederick Forsyth
While We Still Live—Helen MacInnes
On Becoming a Person—Carl R. Rogers
Phases: The Spiritual Rhythms of
Adult Life—Bernard Lievegoed
Day of the Jackal—Frederick Forsyth
The Infinite Power of the Mind—Lauro Trevisan
The Separation of Lovers—Igor Caruso
Juan Salvador Gaviota—Richard Bach

The Great Mysteries of Humanity—I.
C. Lisboa & R. P. Andrade
The Celestine Prophecy—James Redfield
Holocaust—Gerald Green
Churchill as Warlord—Ronald Lewin
The Journey to the East—Herman Hesse
Great Anecdotes of History—Nair Lacerda
The Makers of the Modern World, vol. 6
Brazil, a Land of the Future—Stefan Zweig
Man's Search for Himself—Mollo Ray
Technical Course in Real-Estate
Transactions—Joáo da Silva Araújo
The Ice Age—Margaret Drabble
In the Domain of Mediumship—Francisco Cândido Xavier

25. By phone

"Hi, this is Luciana. Leave a message after the tone."
Slut! Bitch! Whore! Cock-chasing tramp! Slut! Slut! Slut!

"Hi, this is Luciana. Leave a message after the tone."
Slut! Back-alley slag! Two-bit whore! I'm a decent woman! I don't deserve this! You cocksucking minx! Whore! (*Pause*)
But God is good . . . you'll get yours, bitch! Cunt! Slag! Slag!

"Hi, this is Luciana. Leave a message after the tone."
What do you get out of this, eh, bitch? (*Pause*)
What do you get from seeing other people suffer, what?

(*Pause*) From seeing a son cry . . . not understanding why . . . his father . . . spends nights away . . . or the rebellious daughter . . . the mother (*voice breaking into sobs*) Daddy's . . . seeing someone . . . else (*furious*) You slut! Slut! What do you get from this? You back-street whore! Whore!

"Hi, this is Luciana. Leave a message after the tone."
You know he's not what he used to be, don't you? That he's getting old? Well? Have you thought about that? That you're twenty years younger than him? (*Pause*) That might not make such a difference now, right? But it will, when he's sixty . . . he'll be just useless junk to you then . . . and you?

"Hi, this is Luciana. Leave a message after the tone."
Now he leaves a pool of piss on the floor. . . . Not the odd drop on the seat, which would be normal enough . . . but a whole puddle . . . as if . . . as if the stream didn't have the umpf anymore, see? as if the stream lacked umpf. . . .

"Hi, this is Luciana. Leave a message after the tone."
And did you know he doesn't shit in the middle of the bowl? Serious . . . I always know when it's him who's used the bathroom . . . his turd slides down the porcelain into the water . . . leaves a sort of snail's trail. . . . You lift the lid and you see it . . . the track, hardened . . . stuck there . . . stinking. . . . And the son of a bitch pig doesn't even clean it. . . .

"Hi, this is Luciana. Leave a message after the tone."

And if you need anything done around the house, forget it. . . . Don't count on him. . . . He doesn't lift a finger. . . . He couldn't even wash a cup to save his life. . . . Oh, worse thing is he puts sourdough in his milk . . . it sort of coagulates and leaves a ring around the rim . . . disgusting! (*Pause*) Change a lightbulb? Hammer in a nail . . . ? Sheez!

"Hi, this is Luciana. Leave a message after the tone."
You're still young . . . you'll learn. . . . (*Pause*) But take some advice, just one little tip: all that stuff he appears to be, he's none of it. . . . (*Pause*) In the early days, when you still don't really know each other . . . it's a bed of roses . . . because we only show our good sides . . . but then . . . later . . . when you start living together . . . the routine sucks! (*Pause*) The stench of his cigarettes . . . the sleep in his eyes . . . his bad humor . . . problems at work . . . kids driving you nuts . . . relatives . . . his mother! (*Pause*) Then you discover he likes to turn in early and that once in bed no one can make so much as a squeak or he goes ballistic. . . . That he hates the soaps . . . That he hates going out . . . That you can't say a word to him when he's watching a Palmeiras game . . . That Saturday afternoons are off-limits because he has to meet his pals for beers . . . to shoot the breeze . . . (*Pause, voice cracking*) So . . . then you really . . . I mean really . . . start to see who . . . who the man you're sleeping with really is. . . .

26. Diapers

The security guard, a big black guy wide as a door, impeccable in his black suit, discreetly approached the skinny, boney black guy in a tattered white T-shirt filthy jeans and sneakers with worn soles, who'd been pushing a supermarket cart around for over half an hour—five packs of disposable diapers and a tin of baby's milk.

The security guard, a big black guy wide as a door, impeccable in his black suit, had been told by his boss, watching the aisles on an array of CCTV cameras, to check out the skinny, boney black guy in a tattered white T-shirt filthy jeans and sneakers with worn soles and chipped front teeth, who, having swept ten packs of diapers into his supermarket cart, had taken up position near the checkouts as if he were trying to pick someone out among the customers.

The security guard, a big black guy wide as a door, impeccable in his black suit, discreetly followed the skinny, boney black guy in a tattered white T-shirt filthy jeans and sneakers with worn soles and chipped front teeth, who, with swift arithmetic, returned three packs of diapers to the shelf and grabbed a tin of powdered milk, before wheeling his cart over to the express checkout, his eyes scanning the labyrinths all the while.

The security guard, a big black guy wide as a door, impeccable in his black suit, was pretty sure it was a false call when he saw the skinny, boney black guy in a tattered white T-shirt filthy jeans and sneakers with worn soles and chipped front teeth, lost in thought, putting the powdered milk back on the shelf and carefully studying a bottle+bib+pacifier combo, the cheapest on the rack. Eyes down, he replaced two diaper packets, fingered out a tally, brow lined with concentration, and, resolute, arched over his cart, made for the express checkout. Halfway there, an about-face. The bottle+bib+pacifier combo went back onto the shelf, replaced in the cart by the tin of powdered milk, the sums undone, palms sweating, he makes a beeline for the checkout for the "elderly, pregnant, and people with special needs," sure the oppressive weight would soon be lifted from his chest.

The security guard, a big black guy wide as a door, impeccable in his black suit, discreetly approached the skinny, boney black guy in a tattered white T-shirt filthy jeans and sneakers with worn soles who'd been wheeling his cart around for about a half an hour now—five packs of diapers and a tin of baby's milk. Startled by the polite but sudden arm-twist, the order came to him through clenched teeth, *You're comin' with me . . . not a squeak now, ya hear! If you make a fuss I'll snap you in half!* And the boss, *Nab! I've had my eye on you for ages!* he says, waving at the monitors feeding footage from the video cameras spread about the supermarket as he frogmarches him to a small room, with cold cement floor, where, stripped to his shorts, he tries to explain, for the love of god, that his wife's just given birth, to a boy, no name yet, but if he had his way it'd be Tiago, and that he's out of work, so he tried to take out a loan, but times are tough! loan sharks, that's all that's left, so he decided to come here, put some diapers and baby's milk in a cart, who knows? expose his situation to the public, maybe someone would offer to foot the tab, it's not much, they'd get their money back, bill on bill, as soon as he got himself sorted, but, here's the thing, he chickened out; never in his life! Beg! Hell no! hard times, yeah, hard times. The head of security, sitting on a swivel chair, looks up at the big black guy wide as a door, impeccable in his black suit, *Hats off! Have to admit the guy is good!* and dialed the cops. The skinny, boney black guy in a tattered white T-shirt filthy jeans and sneakers with worn soles started to holler that he wasn't a thief and made for the door only to be clocked on the head and not having eaten anything so far that Tuesday, he lay in a dizzy swoon on the ground, dimly hearing the swirl of spiel *These people are all the same . . . same old story every time . . . decent folk . . . honest . . . hardworking. . . . You know why he's so worked up? You know why? Cuz he's probably got a rap sheet this long . . . man, if there's one thing I can recognize a mile away it's a newjack . . . a punk . . . I can smell 'em. . . .* And the big black guy wide as a door, impeccable in his black suit, thinks to himself, with a snarl, man, that Souza is one bitchin cold-ass motherfucker!

27. The preacher

Mulatto, of indefinite age (somewhere between twenty and thirty), sky-blue suit, loose pants, long jacket, cream-colored shirt, yellow tie with a shoal of tiny colored fish on it, the simple gaze of one who carries pocketsful of truth, like candies. He steps off the electric bus, off the mark. On the corner, the shoe shiners of Barão de Paranapiacaba Street signal the proximity of the place revealed to him in dream. Before his eyes, large and chaotic, Sé Square stretches indolently. Alone, he skirts the mouths of the escalators constantly plying the depths of the subway. To the left, the steps of Sé Cathedral, with their layabouts, junkies, glue-sniffing, crack-smoking street urchins, bums, drunks, pickpockets, cell-phone thieves, headbangers, retirees, old fogies. Weak at the knees, he closes his eyes, *Where is my divine inspiration?* Not much time, soon the words will have to come, *How am I to speak to hearts of stone?* The black leather of his Bible sweats the palms of his trembling hands. "Brothers!" he stumbles into the bustle, into the voices, the honking horns, the engines, the bawling peddlers, the blare of music. He breathes the exhaust fumes. "Brothers!" he cries, meeting with startled, curious glances from passersby. "Brothers!" he repeats, wearily. "I have walked a long, long way to get here," *Help me, Lord. Make words sprout from my mouth.* "I look around . . . and what do I see?" *What* do *I see?* "I see the suffering of those disillusioned by life. I see the pain of those who have no past . . . no present . . . and no future. . . ." An old man with sharp blue eyes stops to listen. An office boy, baseball cap turned back, plastic folder packed with papers under his right arm, watches mockingly. "You, brother—and you, sister—who are sad, anguished, lost . . . It is to you that I speak. . . . It is to you that Jesus has sent me . . . to bear witness to my salvation." Sweat clings to his entire body. Clouded vision reveals four men and three women. The kid in the baseball cap slinks away, his ears connected to a Walkman; old blue-eyes stands firm, his face a spray of blood vessels. *Lord, I am weak. Lord, do not forsake me.* His shirt soaked through, his tie knot like a noose, "Brothers, the man you see before you is a man reborn, rescued from hell . . . an ignorant fool who lived in the valley of darkness . . . I, brothers and sisters, I did not know the Lord. . . . In my blindness, I envied the rich! Yes, I wanted to be one of them! Big car . . . fancy clothes . . . all the best food and drink . . . Date all the most sought-after women . . . So . . . to achieve that, for a long time . . . I stole . . . I robbed . . . and even . . ." Dizzy, he steps toward the semicircle of listeners, fifteen, maybe twenty people? "What was I looking for, brothers? There was an emptiness inside . . . I used prostitutes, snorted cocaine, drank imported whiskey. . . . And the day after, what was left of it? Nothing! Absolutely nothing! So to fill that void I did it all again: I stole some more . . . robbed more people . . . and . . ." *Deliver me from sin. Deliver me, Lord, from this prison.* . . . He sets his Bible down on the edge of a flower box behind him, moves toward a woman with a child in tow, peering restlessly through a stand of legs, and asks if she wouldn't mind holding his suit jacket for just a moment. Turning back to the gathering, he unbuttons his cuffs and rolls up his sleeves, displaying his arms: tattooed from the shoulder down with irregular parallel lines that branch into deltas at the knuckles, as if the marks upon his skin signaled others, deeper, running in the dark, turning weak muscles into powerful winged claws. He buttons his cuffs back up, pulls on his suit jacket, "Thank you, sister," and picks up his Bible. "Yes, brothers. I have known torture . . . humiliation . . . I have seen death . . . in the eyes . . . of those . . ." *My Lord . . . the pain . . . again . . . I can't . . . my Lord* . . . "A monster . . . brothers! A monster . . . that's what I was." "Oooh, a monster!" screech some kids, in false falsetto, as they barge through the gathering with files of paperwork. "But . . . praise the Lord . . . Jesus . . . Jesus . . . saved me. He saved me from the bottom of the bottom of the pit . . . so that I might spread . . . the good news." "Hallelujah, brother!" mocks a passerby, coaxing laughter. The dirty handkerchief with its embroidered *J* daubs his sweating brow. "Brothers!" he bellows, kneeling, arms raised skyward, as a helicopter beats the air, he holds his Bible aloft in his right hand, his face tilted toward the Most High, eyes clenched shut, blotting out the midday sun, "Brothers! Lift up your thoughts to God . . . pray with me, brothers! My Lord, I . . . your humble servant . . . I am nothing,

Lord . . . mere dust blown in the wind . . . I ask thee, I implore thee, look upon our brothers who suffer, Lord . . . upon those who climb without hope to the tops of buildings . . . upon those who have not the strength to resist the mire of drugs . . . upon those, jobless, who succumb to temptation . . . upon those who have lost everything and those who never had anything to lose . . . look down upon the anonymous who languish unseen. Lord, Lord, free us from the war . . . that rages . . . within . . . within . . . within each . . . and every . . ." and the words stick in his throat, stayed by a crushing weight, as if a monolith had fallen across his chest drowning out the afternoon symphony
exploding it in blackouts
for seconds? minutes? a pair of shoes appears a pair of worn-out trainers approaches, he sees cigarette butts fallen leaves plastic cups pigeons napkins sweet wrappers a pool of piss "You alright?" "Yes, I'm fine. . . . Fine . . ." he gets to his feet, slaps down his pants and jacket, his handkerchief locates a sliver of blood on the crown of his head as he staggers toward Largo de São Francisco and his stomach burns and his head pounds *Lord, I am not worthy*

28. Business

The navy-blue, bulletproofed Mercedes double-parks outside Graduate School and a boy pops from the scrum of uniforms and jumps inside, muting the noisy preamble to a hysterical afternoon—boisterous kids, neurotic parakeets, rumbling car engines. He burrows into his father, creasing his lead-gray Armani suit and depositing his filthy schoolbag at his feet, and receives an awkward pat on the head in return, a gentle tousling of his soft black hair.

—Told you I'd come, didn't I?

Haydn (Fourth String Quartet in G Minor, opus 76, number 1) conducts the car, a frigid capsule, eighteen degrees Celsius, an oasis in the lunchtime chaos.

—Congratulations!

And he gives the lad a playful slap on his hairless leg.

—Twelve! Yes siree. . . . Twelve years of age!

The air-conditioning is uncomfortable for the boy.

—So how's school?

—Cool I, guess. . . .

—That's my boy. . . . Hey, Nakamura, can't you take another route, this is going nowhere. . . . Right . . . Ehm . . . And is everything set for the party Saturday?

—Uh-uh.

Red light. He watches the street bum at a woman's windshield, and the woman, pinned in on all sides, harassed and anxious, clutching the steering wheel; an old lady comes up pushing a bouquet of jaded roses; a guy files by peddling cheap tools; another selling tea towels, "embroidered by hand"; and another sweating buckets under a Styrofoam box of bottled water; a girl with a baby in her arms demands spare change; undernourished urchins vie for windshields, wielding squeegees and water bottles; teenage girls with smiley thighs slide real-estate fliers through the chinks of windows.

—So, says the father, fumbling for the loose thread of lost conversation. So did they sing "Happy Birthday"? Did they?

Ah . . . good . . . And . . . to celebrate . . . you know where we're going? Just the two of us (**his cell phone rings**)
He takes out the phone, turns awkwardly toward the window, instantly recognizes the number on the screen and sends it through to voice mail.
—How about a Big Mac?
—A Big Mac?
—Sure, why not?
—We're going to McDonald's?
—Sure are!
—Yes, yes!
The boy punches the air and throws himself round his father's neck.
—Cool, Dad!
—And then . . . Nakamura, did you set up the . . . the surprise . . . like I said? All set? I think you're going to like this. . . .
—What is it, Dad?
—Guess . . .
He frowns thoughtfully.
—A guitar? It's a guitar, isn't it?
—Nooooo . . .
—No? So what is it then?
—It's something you really, really want. . . .
—Something I really want, and it's not a guitar. Hmmm . . .
—Think . . . think . . .
—I know, it's a racing kart. It's a kart, right? Right?
His cell phone rings again, he pulls out the phone, turns toward the window, the heavy gold watch strap recognizes the number, the Breitling wristwatch lowers his voice, "I can't talk now. I'll

call you in . . . (he looks at his son, who is grinning with anticipation at the envy he's about to cause in his classmates) in . . . five minutes, okay?"

While the boy gets in line, "No, just some chicken nuggets and a Diet Coke for me." He heads for the parking lot to make the call.

At the baptism, his shoes took him into a corner of the nave, away from the jumble of voices—godparents, relatives, guests—and into a tiny side chapel off the transept, where the Dead Christ lay torn and bloodied, the pain sunken in his features, devoid of serenity, only revolt and melancholy, regurgitations from a difficult gangland. Lightheaded, perched on a kneeler, he gave in, he agreed, the boy would know everything, the little pagan, he'd tell him everything when he reached the age of twelve. By then, he felt, he'd be able to understand, he'd have discernment. However, watching him now through the glass, his mouth smeared ketchup-red and mustard-yellow, those certainties were being shredded in the wind. What if he damned him for it? What if he *didn't*? How was he to explain that . . . that he wasn't proud of . . . of his . . . business . . . ? He wanted to spare the boy the "humiliations" he'd known, the gibes from his night-school classmates, a decent sleep at the mercy of his wallet, exhausted after a day hacking cattle and swine at his uncle's butcher's; the same bags under his eyes had accompanied him down the crooked corridors at Law School, and as he lugged books along with him on the bus ride home. All that sacrifice, and if he hadn't taken the leap he'd have ended up just like his parents—God keep them—and his kids too, probably: nobodies. From jailhouse lawyer, "people, contacts," small services, favors

really—a throwaway gun for a client—to brokering gunrunning deals out of Miami. He was a visionary, the lines on the palm of his soft, manicured hand read
ports, airports, clandestine airstrips, bridges,
rivers, roadways
Austrian Glock pistols and Israeli Jerichos
Israeli Uzi submachine guns and Argentine FMs
Russian AK-47s, American Ruger 223s, Swiss SIG Sauers
AR-15s, M-16s
He sits in front of his son, a nugget dipped in barbecue sauce,
—So, how's it taste?

29. Paradise

The boy didn't like it much, but compared to two months back, it was paradise. Curled up in a hole on Henrique Schaumann, face dirty from the boot soles of cops, the point of some crackhead's switchblade prodding his tuberculate chest, wondering who'd come calling next, the hooded goons who tread soft and hit hard, or the rich-kid delinquents who douse them in gasoline and flick a match. Now he's lying on a mattress, a thin one, but with clean sheets, a trim blanket, perfumed pillow. And if the darkness devours his sleep, you can only blame the sidewalks, because the only noise you hear in the apartment is the drippity-drop of the leaky faucet—if only he had some pliers and a new washer. And if he doesn't eat, you can only blame his last meal, still sludge on stomach lining, because the German dishes it up, hot lunches every day, and there's always leftovers at dinner. The problem is the walls, the fact that he can't go out, that sucks! Behind closed doors, he's got everything he needs: cold water, TV, stereo, radio (remote control in his hand, he's gonna be a DJ when he grows up). But the hours drag by: he sleeps, gets up, takes a whiz, takes a dump, eats, watches kiddies' TV, the cartoons, the news, eats, watches the reruns, the afternoon flick, the back-to-back soaps, the evening news, the night-owl session, then takes a whiz, takes a dump, hits the sack. Every now and then, the German'll say, Work tomorrow, available for hours on end, a real bummer. The German, Gunther. There's a lock on the phone, incoming calls only. He ripped out the intercom which he chucked, broken, into a damp cabinet under the sink. He sometimes locks himself in his room with his computer, restricting the kid's movements to the sitting room and kitchen, little more than a fitted wardrobe, really. And when he says there'll be work tomorrow, he arrives the next day with some friends, some women, and some girls, who don't even have tits yet, and they snort coke, drink, take off their clothes, and the gringos take pictures and film them rubbing off each other and licking each other out, and the German and the boy go at them hard, taking turns,

The German said there are pictures of me online, that someday he'll show them to me, says he deposits my fee in a savings account and that

The big hand mangles my shoulder he could crush my skull if he wanted to he observes to his friends: but the worst part is being kept prisoner one of these nights I'll get a toe on the windowsill the next floor down then jump onto the marquee I've been thinking it through, have it all figured

30. The continuous old-fella

The continuous old-fella, the yellow and whites of his eyes, ran the tap to wet his heavy hands, soaped them up and slowly started scrubbing, saying as he did, not so much to the acquaintance at the adjacent sink, or to the bike courier swaying over the urinal, as to anyone who cared to listen, anyone at all in the rancid restroom,
the wife just rang . . . says there's one hell of a shootout on our street . . . she was calling from behind the sofa, pulled up against the wall for cover, terrified she was gonna take a stray bullet in the head, poor thing . . . all worried, she was . . . said for me not to turn up home wearing the suit, as they might take me for a detective or something . . . and I thought to myself . . . what tripe! Who the hell could take me for a detective? But, you know, bless her . . . she's got a point . . . what's a guy to do? I'll leave the jacket on the back of my seat, stick the tie in the pocket . . . just leave them there . . . what's the bother? No one's gonna touch them . . . and I'm gonna wear them again tomorrow anyways . . . may as well please the missus . . . she's getting on, poor dear . . . and we . . .
Then the continuous old-fella realizes he's just washing water down the drain, so he rinses and closes the tap with an embarrassed grimace, dries his hands in some paper towels and leaves the restroom, eyes down, the dead river, the indifferent cars, the futuristic buildings, the dark curtain on the horizon, *the old dear, bless her*

31. Faith

PRAYER TO SAINT EXPEDITUS

FEAST DAY APRIL 19. CELEBRATED ON THE 19TH DAY OF THE MONTH

IF YOU ARE IN A PICKLE AND NEED URGENT HELP, CALL ON SAINT EXPEDITUS, THE PATRON SAINT OF MATTERS IN NEED OF SPEEDY RESOLUTION; ANYTIME IS ENOUGH TIME TO BESEECH HIS HELP

Prayer: Saint Expeditus, patron of causes just and urgent, intercede on my behalf before Our Lord Jesus Christ, help me in this hour of affliction and despair. You, who were a holy warrior; you, who are the saint of the wretched; you, who are the saint of the despairing, the saint of urgent causes, I ask your protection, your assistance, give me courage and serenity. Expedite my request. (*state your request*) Saint Expeditus, help me through these times of need, protect me from those who would harm me, protect my family, expedite my request with the greatest speed.

RESTore my peace and tranquility. Saint Expeditus, I shall be grateful till the end of my days and shall spread your name to all who have faith. My deepest thanks. (*recite the Our Father, the Hail Mary, and make the sign of the cross*)

I had a thousand copies of this printed and distributed to give thanks and also to spread word of the graces of the great Saint Expeditus. Place your own order immediately after making your request.

Printed by LRS Productions

Telephones: 3368-6096 and 3204-1744—R$38.00 per thousand

Free home delivery, anywhere in Brazil

32. Kitchen

The motor of the Consul Contest 28 refrigerator, off-white, shakes the kitchen from its silence. The blue walls, the color of angels' robes, is offset by the red ceramic floor tiles, laid against the will of the lady of the house, who leaves for work in the dying hours of the night, so she's never seen the tiny dust particles basking in the glow of the first rays of dawn light filtering through the cracked frosted panes of the louvers.

On top of the refrigerator:

a Walita mixer, rarely used

a collegiate boldline spiral notebook (8 1/2 x 11 inch paper, 96 sheets, 7/16 inch line space): Minnie's Ball on the cover; on the first page, in careful calligraphy, ***Recipe Book***, nothing else inside;

A Ventamatic fan blows the turn of the century at the Ferrari wall clock

A girl, five or six years old, with a frightened pout, 50 x 50 cm, black and white, watches the ants

climbing the far wall

A spoon and fork, the handles painted black with red details, tagged in white, respectively: *Me* *You* swoon on the metal table covered with a white plastic lattice-hem tablecloth, four wine-colored metal chairs, in a gnarl

On the wall:

The Last Supper in high relief with faux aged-iron finish on wood (9 x 15 inches)

A Renoir's *Pink and Blue*, stained, faded, framed in wood

A napa leather armchair

A light brown plywood rack, with

a Frahm three-in-one

a Philips laser CD player cd 165

a telephone book

an Ibratel telephone

two photographs

one of a boy, aged two to three

stuffed into yellow-stamped blue dungarees

over a Parmalat lion shirt

a plaster manger with straw roof

In the drawer:

a photo album, the Swiss Alps

a Bible, João Ferreira de Almeida trans.

two identical flowerpots

two identical wilting flowers

On the bar:

Quinta das Macieiras cider

Prestige sparkling wine

A Wein Zeller dry white wine

Cereser cider

Canção red moscato table wine
Contini vermouth bianco
White Horse scotch whiskey (knockoff)
Liebfraumilch white table wine
Records (vinyl):
Jairzinho & Simony
Só pra Contrariar
Cardume (Nenhum de Nós)
Inimigos do Rei
. . . *Em Algum Lugar* . . . (Roberto Leal)
O Dono do Mundo (International)
Great Stars, Great Hits

On the reddish-brown plywood stand:
1 Panasonic NV-SD 435 video recorder
1 Semivox television
4 Kaiser beer glasses
1 jar
1 ice tongs
5 wineglasses
1 plaster duck
1 porcelain vase with plastic flowers
1 stainless-steel ashtray
1 stainless-steel tray:

Memento of the silver wedding anniversary
of Jacira & Haroldo
07/03/99

•

9 CDs:

Grupo Molejo—*Não Quero Saber de TiTiTi*
Sambas de Enredo '98
Molejo—*Brincadeira de Criança*
Leandro & Leonardo—(*Um Sonhador*)
Banda Eva Live
Raça Negra
Terra Samba ao Vivo e a Cores
Só pra Contrariar
Xuxa—*Só Faltava Você*

1 jar of orange compote

33. Life before death

The old man lives in apartment 205 along with his eldest, a single mother, separated; his teenage granddaughter; and his youngest, a goodfornothing of around thirty, give or take. There are other sons and daughters, who only come around when his health fails, humming his cubicle for the nectar of hate, starting up fights for the hell of it, sparring, ragging, then, zip, they're gone; they don't seem to get along at all. In the shadows of the building's moldy corners he takes his torn Kendall compression stockings for a walk, the sheath concealing the pallor of his boney body. The daughter, a hard worker, sweats to make ends meet: she keeps the creditors at bay by incrementing her wages with her father's meagre pension. The old man knows he's a dead weight, but he draws consolation from the fact that he serves some good at least.

Every now and then the cops come around. The son, a drug addict, gets aggressive when he can't spot a fix and goes berserk if riled. He's smacked the old man around a few times, even put him in intensive care once. The eldest tries to intervene, but what can she do? That time, out of sheer rage, she chucked her brother's entire wardrobe out the window, piece by piece, and watched as the clothes flapped and glided to the parking lot below. As payback, she was left with polka dots of iodine where he gouged out lumps of skin with the point of his knife, screaming I'll cut you up, bitch, you fucking whore!

The granddaughter is a good kid. She's got a bit of a chip on her, but teenagers always do. With her it's all tattoos, piercings, secondhand clothes, dyed streaks in her hair, a cigarette, then another, attitude. Sure, the old man's a nag, always going on about something, but then the volume of her three-in-one does make the walls shudder, and it bothers the neighbors. But she's ballsy, the minx. If they complain, she goes to the window and yells out Call the cops, assholes! Sons-uv-bitches. I wanna see the pigs wastin' their time on shit like this, hardeharharhar! She does have a softer side too, though, justice be done. She's been seen, all sweet and helpful, propping the old man up and walking him over to Block B, where pale sunlight visits the nothing-else-to-do crew that ends up blown into that corner, playing wagers, draughts, crazy eights, spoons, dominoes, bingo. But she's also been known to drop gloves with her mom, and not just once or twice. The two of them going at it in the hallway, a real spectacle! The other day the mother was seen in shades, with scratch marks on her neck and shoulders and bite marks down her arms, her mouth a grimace of shame, while the young one wears her bruises like medals.

Despondent, the old man whiles away his days in the musty room he shares with the son. Lying facedown on his top bunk, he looks out at the backside of Block C, a caking yellow wall, where the kids play football, ride bikes and skateboards, shoot the breeze, make plans, scrap, curse each other out, laugh, listen to music on massive portable stereos, and smoke like chimneys.

Some days ago he came knocking on my door, all disheveled, wispy white hair stinking of coal tar, and he asks me through the wonky dentures in his gummy mouth if I have any books on life after death. I found it strange, because we're only on nodding terms. I see. . . . Are you a Spiritist? His yellow eyeballs scan for some refuge in his hands, which are fidgeting with the shirttail of his white-and-blue-striped PJs, reeking of sweat, Well, please come in. . . . He takes two steps and stops, as I work my way through the book spines on the shelf, *Heaven and Hell*, Allan Kardec, I hold it out to him, and he takes it, starts to leaf. Yeah . . . I think . . . , he whispers. If you'd like to borrow it . . . So he turns around and shuffles his worn trainers, stuffed with his green feet, back down the dark hallway. . . .

34. That woman

that woman who drags herself scarecrow down the streetavenues of morumbi hair sticking out like that gelled by filth her eyes wild and wired wrinkled skin bruised sore-pocked legs arms black fingernails dress in tatters
that woman who drags herself scarecrow down the streetavenues of morumbi babbles and dribbles foams at the edges of flat lips dead stare hands that dangle gesticulate legs in a bendy bow

that woman who drags herself scarecrow down the streetavenues
of morumbi bothersome asking for spare change demanding
febrile irritated weepy spitting questions of varying intensities
that woman who drags herself scarecrow down the streetavenues
of morumbi oblivious to the rats and the roaches to the rain or
the sun the runoff in the gutters to the flip-flops shoes trainers
cops oblivious
that woman who drags herself scarecrow down the streetavenues
of morumbi
wasn't always like that
no
she wasn't
:
she became like this one day, when, at the expected time, her daughter of eleven didn't come home from school, didn't come rushing into the kitchen, panting, Mom! that night, and the next morning, her bed, her starched sheets unslept, and the next day, and the day after that, nothing nothing nothing and she did the humiliating rounds of police stations hospitals correction centers ERs morgues tracing and retracing the route from home to school to home to school knocking on doors looking for clues signs intuitions
until
one night
they knock on her window, they're calling her, public telephone, run, legs wobbling, heart, someone . . . some information . . . maybe . . . her? **Honey?**
On the other end sobbing
panic

She hears the voice **Honey? Where . . . where are you? Honey? Where?**
—she hears voices— silence
falls to her knees on the sidewalk the palms of her hands seared into the concrete strewn with matchsticks cigarette butts bottle tops gobs of spit and she crawls off after
the voice
where did it come from?
where?
and she dragged herself scarecrow down alleys and streets
and they nailed up the windows and doors of her shack
and she was never seen again in paraisópolis
never
again
neither one
nor the other

35. Everything ends

Luciano ventrally decubitus on the mattress eyes fixed on the plaster coving of the ceiling the TV running a cartoon in a few years the apartment will need repainting the beams reinforcing the leaks in the bathroom ceiling which have already picked at the mortar between the tiles will have seeped through to the water pipes hardening the wiring causing short circuits and the ruined, condemned building will be overrun with squatters junkies loons dealers fighting over the turf and everything will end because everything does
and this room in which

Luciano ventrally decubitus on the mattress eyes fixed on the plaster coving of the ceiling watches a cartoon on TV will be rubble with seeping sewage carpet torn up rotting walls scrawled with graffiti the windows cracked and a silence will settle where now there is the rumble of cars and buses and sirens of police cars fire engines and the gaggle of voices and rattle of gas trucks and hollering of fruit sellers corncobs kids playing ball on the hot asphalt and babies crying in some window and the husband the wife the parents the kids and babies stifling in rooms with cable TV strange noises from the apartment upstairs with furniture moving marbles pinging and rolling footsteps in the corridor late-night phones ringing cell phones ringing interphones, nothing, only doors slamming doors banging slamming doors

and none of this will remain none of it and the whole neighborhood will be a wasteland dead space under every dead streetlight on each corner bars dead behind half-closed shutters each flat townhouse slum each cat dog sack of trash and it will all have been in vain são paulo fallen asunder and abandoned by one and all a ghost town like in old black-and-white westerns he rents from the video store and watches from the edge of his bed eating microwave popcorn and drinking coca-cola

and he thinks

for what

why

if some thousands of years from now the earth will succumb to a hecatomb and cease to spin cold inert

and the sun will swallow itself a ball of hydrogen that devours its own stomach

what for

if it all ends
everything
everything lost in an instant
the guy at the traffic lights takes a fright
shoots
and the guy bleeding out over the steering wheel the engine running
the people furious in the traffic jam
he
holding up the traffic
the people behind him all livid
honking
honking
furiously livid

36. Read Psalm 38

read psalm 38
three days in a trot
three times a day
make two difficult requests
and one impossible
announce on the third day
wait and see what happens on the fourth

37. Party

Idalina tiptoed into the room, as if there were any need for that, as if silence would have made any difference, now that her friend feels nothing, absolutely nothing at all. However, that's how she entered, out of respect if anything, to avoid bumping into things in the half dark—five whole hours out there, another afternoon down the drain, violets wilting in caked earth in butter pots: the navy bedsheet improvised as a curtain lets in puddles of lackluster sun.

The tiny room, with its stench of illness, displays: a lamp with a blue shade on a bedside table, the portrait of a Holocaustic baby, an empty glass, pill foils, the thin white arms of a plaster Christ contrasting against the dank dark green walls, a brittle plywood wardrobe, a threadbare woven rug on the worn wood-tile floor. And, stretched out on the coarse, sackcloth sheets, abandoned, her skeleton protruding through her gray, parchment skin, is she.

Idalina was there to honor her friend's last (and only) wish: to make her up. Vain to the end! Be laid out looking like this: emaciated, desiccated, rough-hewn, cadaveric, and bald? Like some African droughtlander on the nine-o'clock news? No way! Sighing, she dragged a stool to the bedside, turned on the lamp (why not open the window? for fear of offending now useless eyes?), and opened the makeup case on the bed. She'd given her word and now she had to honor it. They'd known each other since the age of eleven, their ID cards listing the same age, twenty-nine in August. Leo, the pair of them, her ascendant in Virgo, her friend's in Capricorn. They met in sixth grade at night school, in Rio Pequeno. Idalina helped her mother out making dumplings, kibbes, *sfihas*, rissoles, pastels, and pastries, and the friend insisted on going with her to deliver them for birthday parties, weddings, engagement parties, farewell gatherings. There was always a party being thrown somewhere, and they found it impressive back then the way different people took part in different ways, the drinkers and eaters having fun, the uniformed waiters roaming with trays among crowds of guests, offering snacks and sweets.

I want to be a doctor when I grow up, so I can help my fellows, that's what she used to write in her school essays. She kept a black-covered diary, under lock and key, which she once allowed Idalina to take a peek at, all those silly afflictions, little joys, dumb sorrows, the humdrum happenings of Jardim D'Abril, her father away at work, her mother busy bringing up the seven of them, and she didn't get along with the eldest, or with the younger ones, who didn't give a monkey's, so she clung to Idalina, her snacks their excuse to stick together. Not even the eighth-grade diaspora made them part, and they remained close throughout the beautician's course at Senac. Idalina got a job at a parlor in Center Norte shopping mall and settled out in Jardim Brasil. In the meantime her friend met a guy at a dance hall in Pinheiros—"What do you think? Isn't he a dish?"—and wound up in one of the thousands of bare-brick, concrete-slab-roofed hovels on the east side of town.

Idalina landed herself a good-paying job at a branch of Soho in Vila Madalena, where the tips are generous, and got occasional wind of her friend—pregnant, then the baby, nearly six pounds, forty centimeters long, the husband a skirt-chasing profligate who squandered her cash on blow

everything she earned from manicures and pedicures

hairdressing in a backyard shack in Parque São Lucas

everything she earned as a washerwoman and babysitter
everything she earned selling popsicles at the projects in Sapopemba
and then he'd smack her around for all her trouble
his deadbeat friends sitting pasha in the sitting room
the cops raiding the house, the shame of it.
When the boy took ill, vomiting and passing water, and ended up in the ER, they said it was diarrhea, but when it got worse, she hit the hospitals, morning noon and night, pneumonia, virus, flu, until they did his bloods
"I'm so sorry. . . ."
and . . . if . . . then . . . she . . . yes, most probably . . .
HIV positive, she nearly went nuts with all the thoughts in her head, but, why this ill! The boy, he's not reacting to any ARV, the cocktail just doesn't work
and he only lasted a few more months.
She prayed to all the saints
saint expeditus and saint rita of cassia
saint anthony and saint izildinha
took friar galvão remedies
And she embraced all known creeds
the universal church, church of brasil-for-christ
the assembly of god, the Seventh-day adventists
spiritism macumba candomblé
And she tried every trick
massage
magic conches
bottled tonics

She dredged the very bottom of her savings account, pawned her apartment, bled herself dry looking for miracles she knew never happened at Emílio Ribas Hospital, with all that group help, poor devils, caught the "pest," dying off like flies. So she tracked down Idalina, left a message begging to see her again, even if just one more time.

Idalina went to see her, out of pity, and found the poor wretch abandoned, alone, the scumbag having bolted as soon as the boy got sick; him of all people, the vector, who's probably out there as we speak, sentencing more unsuspecting schmucks to an early death. She looked up some of her family: in Vila das Mercês she contacted her brother, the owner of a dive, who bawled her out of the place, saying, "She's already dead as far as I'm concerned, the tramp, dead! Understand?"; on Francisco Morato, her evangelical sister wouldn't even hear of her, "It's in God's hands now, dear, it's all in the Lord's good hands"; in Jandira, another sister, a cleaning lady, said she didn't give a damn, "I've enough problems of my own"; she couldn't find the eldest or the youngest, and another brother had already kicked the bucket.

So, with a sigh, Idalina set about applying the foundation to the gray skin of her friend's emaciated face, followed by moisturizer, blusher, blue eyeliner, red lipstick, and eye shadow

little by little, her friend, ever so vain, shed twelve years of gray, lightening back to that chirpy girl who dreamed of getting married and becoming a doctor, "so she could help her fellows."

38. The girl

Eight years old, the girl, with lively bituminous eyes and pair of long black plaits, spliced Penelope-like by her mother before leaving for work, at the first rustle of day. The braids, thick and frizzed, are whipped by two broad satin ribbons, which she wears in a dangle.

There's not much meat on her, but she's a healthy cut, lean and elegant. When she walks, her little body intuitively reconstructs the time around it, consciously owning her place in the world.

A loving kid, she's devoted to her mom, and collects colorful words for her dad.

She's a good companion, washes the dishes after breakfast, before riding the bus to school, a twenty-minute squeeze, never out of the driver's sight, who knows her and looks out for her.

Her mother's thirty-two and is a real hoot. She usually gets home from work in the evenings, and she's always got some gossip stowed away in her bag. She's a cleaning lady, paid by the hour, with clients scattered across the city, but no sooner does she put her key in the door than the girl jumps up from the couch to throw herself round her neck. Mommy, did you bring me anything? the soap-opera actors gabbing in the background.

Before catching the minivan to the subway in Vila Carrão, she gets the girl's lunch ready. When she gets back from school, she heats it up, perches herself in front of the TV, and nibbles a bit. Not a big eater, the girl. After that, she turns on the radio and spins a load in the washing machine, then heads out into the tiny paved-over yard to hang the washing out, jabbing each piece on the line with little pink pegs. The ironing's her mom's job. She's not yet able to press out all the rucks, the folds, the creases. . . .

She might not see her dad for days. He's an air-conditioning technician, so he works round the clock. But she does know that he tiptoes into her room in the dark, plants a kiss on her cheek, and tucks in her blankets—she feels his breath. On Sundays, with him all dapper in his best suit, and her mom with her hair bunched into a careful bun, off they go to service at the God Is Love church, where, lined up with the other kids, she ponders the mysteries of other morns hidden in the scriptures.

In fact, she was never supposed to have been conceived, the girl. However hard they tried, her mom just couldn't get pregnant. They started fighting, what with the stress and disappointment, but then the tests came back showing that the husband's semen was low on troops. The pastor held a vigil, and, Praise the Lord! grace was bestowed. It was a rocky pregnancy, though, total repose so as not to lose the baby, so without her earnings, they had to go without, and in this meantime the husband was laid off and had to go looking for odd jobs, nixers, fill-ins, anything, until a brother at the church took him on as an assistant, commission only, fixing air-conditioning units. He was a disaster at first, but soon got the hang of it, now he can fix a unit better than anyone. In the end, only seven months in, along came the girl, consigned to an incubator until she beefed up a bit. So pretty, so smart, so loving, just as mommy and daddy, Sara and Abe, had always dreamed.

The girl sings in the choir on Sunday afternoons. She's already such a good reader that the pastor makes an exception and lets her come up to the pulpit to recite whole passages from the Bible.

39. Diet

Afternoon is the buzz and hum of a floor fan in the small room rigged with makeshift clothes racks and metal shelves stacked with kidswear: swimsuits, bikinis, knickers, blouses, T-shirts, pajamas, undies, shorts, diapers, Bermudas, dungarees, onesies, kiddies' cardigans, caps, and bonnets.

Down the back, behind a desk-cum-checkout, the girl greedily devours the first of three hot dogs her mother, next door down, has just passed over the wall and which her boss, on a brief break from her industrial sewing machine, has just brought to her along with a diet coke.

Tuesday, no customers and almost no money in the drawer, and tomorrow's payday.

The girl, seventeen, is already the sorry owner of stretch marks on her thighs and bust, and cellulite on her butt. But what should she expect, with a Bedouin thirst for sodas? So now she's decided to go on a diet. She gave the money to a friend who knows this pharmacy in Itaquera that sells under-the-counter pills, no questions asked; it costs more, sure, but there's none of the botheration, the doctor's appointments, exams, all that stuff.

Her walkman sits on the dull yellow plywood desk, the wires of her headphones wrapped around the sticky-tape dispenser, as the effusive afternoon settles deep, beyond the capless biros and free cup calendar. Days that go by without a single sale are a worry. Mrs. Sofia's already thinking of shutting up shop, then what?

Licking her blue-nailed fingers, the girl regards the second hot dog. She takes a swig of coke, and lets a dribble escape from the corner of her red lips. She depends on the local custom, on her commission. Mrs. Sofia always approved of her ways, though she never really got a measure of just how convincing she is when closing a sale. The prices are good, but the break-even point is absurd! And the business isn't even legit. Imagine if it was! The boss's husband buys in bulk on Oriente Street, where everything's dirt cheap, then resells the stuff here in São Miguel, and the customers, whether out of ignorance or laziness, keep on buying, even though Brás isn't exactly far away. . . .

The rickety mongrel parked on the pavement outside never budges, just lies there, scratching his sores and fleas, until around three in the afternoon, when, religiously, it drags its scrawny bones to the doorway, begging for leftovers, which it gobbles with the gratitude of the famished.

She dropped out of high school in her first year, to help her parents, she said, what with her dad unemployed and her mother taking care of the house. But things bucked up when her mother started making plush and styrofoam minnies and mickeys, donalds and plutos, sylvesters and tweeties and her dad started hawking carloads of the stuff round the backlands in his opal.

Her sister, a real looker, salesgirl at a classy boutique in the Aricanduva Mall, done up to the nines, clothes stuck to her curves, swanky shoes, a model, she rarely sees her, goes from work straight to university, night course in advertising, gets home late, if she comes home at all, sometimes she'll just ring and say she's staying at a friend's house, up herself, she is! Thinks she's the cat's meow, and her boyfriend, who's a trainee at what the . . . ! gun barrel on her forehead, the guy's voice a growl *Shove the money in here, do it!* Holding out a plastic supermarket bag, and she's got hot dog bun-dough gumming up her tongue, ketchup trickling across her red lips, her hands useless on the tabletop, the cash drawer closed her movements frozen her eyes wide *Put the fuckin' money in the bag!* Impatient, carved-up hands shaking, pale lips trembling beads of sweat on his brow an insecure bark *Just fucking do it!* A voice from upstairs the industrial sewing machine falls silent a cowed yelp a lack of air the trigger bang

40. Where we were at a hundred years ago

The traffic flatlined on the corner of Estados Unidos and Rebouças Avenue. Henrique loosened his tie and turned up the volume on the CD player, Betty Carter spilled into every nook and cranny of his brand-new Honda Civic, the windows rolled up around his unassailable citadel, leaving the world outside, with its heat, smog, tension, bustle and hustle. Filthy raggedy kids squirt water on windshields, slurp it off with squeegees, then stick out their begging little hands, with razor blades concealed between the fingers, stashes of switchblades hidden in bouquets, shards of glass up their sleeves. Raggedy filthy girls lug around rented babies, their innocent little thighs bared, their wispy hair shrouded in vapid dreams. Teenagers dressed in American football shirts hand out real-estate fliers. Butch dudes in American basketball shirts flash revolvers under a ***São Paulo–Miami Nonstop*** billboard covering half of a derelict building, where cats and goo-eyed kids sleep oblivious to the lubricious afternoon.

(Seven-thirty in the evening and the sun still belts down on the fields outside Milan as the train speeds by. Henrique and his wife are sharing a cabin with a thin and smiley elderly couple and a talkative fat off-duty railway guard.
: And you? Where are you coming from?
: From Venice.
: Venice! Did you like it?
: Wow, lots!
: You're from . . . Argentina?
: No way! We're Brazilian.
: Ah! Brazilians! If you don't mind my asking, what brings you here?
: We've come to see my grandfather's homeland. . . .
: Ah, your grandfather is from the region?
: Yes, from Mira.
: Mira! Beautiful place! And where are you headed now?
: Genoa.
: Genoa? But . . . do you have family there? Some special business?
: No . . . it's just that's where my grandfather sailed from, en route to Santos . . . Brazil. . . .
: My oh my, well then . . . So it's Genoa, is it? No, I'm afraid I can't let such a nice young couple, the grandson of a Venetian, go to Genoa. . . .
: But . . . why not?
: Why not? Why, because Genoa is an ugly, horrible city, there's absolutely nothing there to see. . . . What's more, the

Ligurians . . . the Ligurians are a bunch of thieves . . . thieves, the lot of them!

He turns to the old lady, encouraging her to back up his claim.

: It's true. . . . The Ligurians . . . Ligurians are all thieves,. . . .

And the old man, who previously mentioned that he had served in Rome during the Second World War, leans in, whispers:

: There's only one place in Italy worse than Genoa. . . .

And looking out at the landscape streaming by in a blur, concludes:

: Naples.)

)The Venetian Giacomo fell for the Napolitana Maria at a party in Brás. The grandfather had a metal workshop in Barra Funda and everything he earned he splurged on women, honest and dishonest. Perpetually horny, he spent his life dodging goons, debt collectors, and husbands. The grandmother provided for the home and six kids washing, ironing, darning, and filling sausages. Antonio, Henrique's father, turned his mother's weekend stopgap into a business, and soon they owned a meat processing and packing plant, which overran itself and of which not a single brick remains.(

(The Portuguese shuffled in his chair, took another swig of grog, and continued:

: I don't know how you can still stand living in Brazil. Not that I can complain about the place, far be it from me! But there's just no way you can make honest money there anymore. . . . I made mine getting up with the crows and going to bed late at night, because I never did trust the staff. . . . I used to own a bakery, see, until some rich kid I tried to help out started robbing me, the scum!

Henrique's wife got up, whispered, "I'm off to the restroom," and the Portuguese went on:
: I started buying some houses over here, in the village . . . the Portuguese government gives special interest rates to us immigrants . . . so in just two or three years I'll move over for good . . . leave the rest with you guys, who are young, who can still handle that godforsaken mess!)

)The grandfather on his mother's side, a mustachioed tramontane, jet-black slicked-back hair, huge sandpaper hands, an ungainly fellow who cried like a baby whenever he heard Amália Rodrigues, used to lug a cart house to house in Cangaíba, back when the winds still turned in Cangaíba, buying antiques, scrap iron, glass, lead, copper, paper, old furniture, anything that wasn't worth anything anymore. That was how he earned his living. The grandmother, a redneck who couldn't speak the language, would hide herself under the bed, so no one knew where she'd got to. Henrique's mother was born of this miscoupling.(

By the time he realized it, the traffic had chugged on to Henrique Schaumann, where a police car was parked on the sidewalk, where some peddlers were pushing hammocks, toolboxes, flowers, and where Betty Carter modulated the yellow lights flickering on a large electronic panel,

And then the red turned green.

41. Taxicab

Any particular route you'd like, chief? No? So we'll take the quickest one then, which, as you know, is not necessarily the shortest. Here in São Paulo, the shortest route is not always the quickest, am I right? At this time of day . . . five fifteen . . . this time in the evening the city is right about coming to a standstill . . . the expressways, the feeder roads, the junctions, the avenues, the drives, the streets, the lanes, the lot; it's all blocked up, horns honkin'. You know, I once dreamed the whole city stopped, I mean completely. One big traffic jam, a humungous gridlock, like nothin' ever seen before, and no one could move an inch . . . Sounds like somethin' out of a movie, right? Hey, I like the movies, me. I like a good movie. Course, I prefer the old ones. They sometimes still run on TV. Man, there were some great, great actors, I'm thinkin' Tyrone Power, Burt Lancaster. . . . But my favorite was Victor Mature, remember him? He played Maciste, remember? He was damn good, that guy. . . . We've got this portrait of him on the wall back home. Well, it's not exactly a portrait, more a picture from a magazine that the old lady cut out and got framed. Can you believe that? You know what women are like, right . . . ? She knew I was a Victor Mature fan, so she figures I'd like it, you know? She gave it to me for my birthday . . . years ago now. She hung it on the sitting room wall. . . . You reckon I had the balls to take the thing down? Not me. Would you, chief? In fact, once I was at home on my own and I threw it on the floor, broke the glass 'n' all, and I said it was the wind that blew it down, and she believed me, so I figured I'd finally gotten rid of the thing. Wouldn't you know? The very next week there it was again, good as new, can you believe that? She thinks she's doing something to please me, so what's a guy to do? When my daughters were teenagers—they're grown women now, all married, and well-married too, thank Christ—they used to die a death because of that picture. Dad, how lame is that? they said. And their friends would come by and figure it was a relative or somethin', and they'd say: "Who's the fox?" And I had to agree, I mean it was ridiculous, and I said it to the old lady, and she says to me, Claudinor! What the heck, Claudinor! That's me, Claudinor. What the heck, Claudinor! Pretty soon they're gonna fly the coop and it'll be just you and me, two old fogies. You love that portrait, so you go keep it there. . . . Well, end result, if you stop by mine someday, you'll see Victor Mature hanging there on the sitting-room wall! And, you know what? We had this dog once, this fox terrier, and that SOB didn't leave nothin' intact, I mean nothin'. He'd come flying in the front door and go tearing out the back door wagging his tail about, knockin' everythin' over, flowerpots, whole ferns, unsuspectin' children, he even managed to bash the hell out of a Danish biscuit tin we kept on top of the stand. The old lady went nuts, because she used that tin as a money jar. . . . She mended clothes, see, so any darning she did, any Italian slacks she took up, any buttons she sewed or tear she mended, she'd put the money in the tin. . . . But would you believe it? not even the dog could get rid of that damn portrait! So, what can you do? But gettin' back to the movies, for me, the old stuff's the best. These days, it's one bloodbath after another . . . just ass-kickin' the whole time. . . . And every second scene, if you'll pardon the expression, someone's gettin' humped. It's incredible! You go into a video store and there's a whole shelf just with dirty movies. Some of that stuff would make you cringe. It's women with women, women with horses, no kiddin'! Women with dogs, women gettin' gangbanged, jeez! I know, because, just between you and me, we're all flesh and bone, so this one time the old lady went to the son-in-law's house on the coast and I rented one. . . . I couldn't even watch it to the end, pure filth. A guy's gotta be sick, am I right? I mean to feel anythin' watchin' one of those flicks, it's disgusting! A guy's gotta have somethin' wrong with him, sweet jesus! That was the first and the last time I watched any of that rot, let me tell ya. Now, whenever the old lady heads for the coast, I go with her. My son-in-law built a fine house down in Praia Grande, spacious, right on the beach. And he practically built it himself! Yeah, he works in offset at the Estado de São Paulo, and he bought the plot back when he was still single. Back then there were still chickens in the street, can you believe that? Chickens! Well, as he didn't have the money, he walled in the plot and slowly went about laying the foundations, raising the walls. . . . Then, when he and Maria Lúcia got engaged, he sped up the building, went down there every weekend. Every single detail of that house is just him, from the glass shards on the front wall to the colonial roof, the slate flooring to the color of the bathroom tiles, you can see him in it. First-rate stuff! And he's a swell guy, too. He may have gone up in the world, but ain't forgotten where he came from. The house isn't just his, it's the family's . . . in-laws, friends, parents, brothers and sisters. . . . Every weekend there's someone down there, firing up the barbecue. And everyone gets along. Take my word for it: you go there any Saturday of the year, someone will be down there. He has a close family, which is good, see, because mine and the wife's, well, they're not so close. I left home young, still a boy. I came down from the north on the back of a truck. You can't imagine what it was like. . . . I mean, it was just slats of wood for seats, a tarpaulin cover, everyone eatin' out of tins and lunch boxes, sugarcane and manioc flour, day after day on the road, sweet holy mary! But I can't complain, São Paulo's been like a mother to me. As soon as I arrived I found a job as a cleaner in an auto-parts factory in Santo André. And I worked my way up from there, because, in the past, you could still do that, not like today, when there's no work for anyone. Take me, I'm officially retired, but as I have some years left in me, I still do the odd job just to get by, because this is no place for the old. Or for the young, who can't get their first job because they don't have experience. But no one gives them a chance! How are they supposed to get experience if no one will give them a break? In my day, there was such a shortage of labor that you'd barely climbed down off the back of the truck and you were already in your first job. And they trained you too. I even had money. I took the old lady up to Sergipe more than once, to see my hometown, Nossa Senhora das Dores, you won't have heard of it. This one time I piled the whole lot into a Beetle I'd just bought, it was spanking-new, and hit the Rio-Bahia interstate. The girls were already big at this stage, but the wife gets carsick, so she was green in the face the whole way there. All she has to do is sit in a car and she goes all queasy. Now she's got this trick with lemon juice that can just about get her to the coast in one piece, but that trip north, it was pandemonium! The girls have never been back. . . . Which makes me sad, I won't lie; after all, your land is your land, am I right? But I understand. I'm not ignorant, see. They've got nothing in common with that hole. To tell you the truth, I'm not sure even I do anymore. Most of my childhood friends, the people I used to know, have gone away, they don't live there anymore. And the older folks are all dead. Memory's all that's left, but what's memory? The girls had a ball on the way back on the BR-101, cuz it runs along the coast, see. We stopped off at Guarapari, where there's this black sand that's good for rheumatism. The old lady's got these pains in her joints that not even infiltration can contain. So she covered herself up in that sand, with only the face stickin' out. . . . And as I had nothing to do I took myself off to the nearest bar. Maria Perpétua, the eldest, was old enough to look after the younger ones, so I found myself a deck chair on the sand and sat there like a lord drinking beer and eating fried sardines, watching the chicks go by in their bikinis. I was a bit of a cad back then, see . . . a young buck, handsome, gift of the gab. Hardly a week went by I didn't pull a new chick. And I don't mean the paid variety either, not me, not my thing. For me, even today, a girl can't have any, say, ulterior motives, otherwise I just can't, you know. Excuse the wording, but I just can't get it up. Back then I was able to take a month's vacation, I was settled, had my place in Vila Nova Cachoeirinha, the kids were growing up, the eldest, Maria Perpétua, was doing teacher training. . . . So I'd get up to no good . . . fall into temptation big-time . . . I was laid off from the firm I worked in and decided to use the money from my severance fund to open an electronic games arcade in my garage. . . . You won't believe it, chief . . . when it's not meant to be there's nothing doin', you know . . . ? To make room for the arcade, I had to leave the car in the street. It wasn't insured or nothin'. I just had a steering-wheel lock on it. . . . Man, the arcade became a drug sales-point, and then my car got robbed and I went broke! As if overnight, there I was, startin' over again. . . . I took a job driving buses, until I scraped the money together, with the son-in-law's help, to buy a cab license. It wasn't this rank, it was another one, over in Belém. Then I moved to a rank in Lapa, that was a good one. . . . But at home it's like we have two generations, the older girls, Maria Perpétua and Maria do Carmo, who grew up during the better times, who studied, graduated. Maria do Carmo is a lawyer with her own firm, along with a partner, over in Horto. She's single, but she's well-off, with a great apartment nearby. She's even been abroad, can you believe it? She's got the travel bug. She's been on a cruise. I reckon she takes after me, in that sense, gettin' out and about. . . . She gave me a picture of her in the snow, in Bolivia. But, you know, I think she's sort of sad. She never wanted to marry, I think she must have been unlucky in love, got hurt, once bitten, you know . . . ? The wife has a cousin who found out her husband had another family, wife and three kids, and she just stopped eatin', wouldn't drink, refused to walk, quit everything, she withered away, died by degrees. Maria do Carmo's case is different, she was always sort of closed, very reserved, so much so that we never knew her reasons for taking that path. . . . Maria Perpétua graduated as a teacher, got married, she lives in Campo Limpo, where she teaches in a municipal school. She's doin' well, she is. Her husband's a merchant, a nice guy, but a bit of a shyster, I guess you have to be in that line, it's sink or swim, am I right? It goes with the territory. The other two kids grew up during the hard times, Maria Lúcia and Pedro. Neither of them went very far in their studies, but, thank God, that didn't stop them comin' up in the world. Maria Lúcia, the wife of the son-in-law with the house in Praia Grande, she's a housewife, she only studied up to junior high. But she's better off now than her sisters. Pedro has a stall in a fruit-and-vegetable market, he sells bananas—would you believe, chief, there's good money to be made in bananas? Pedro's doing okay, he's got a good place and gives his kids the best of everything, though he's demanding, oh yeah, the eldest is thirteen, but he has to get up at the crack of dawn every weekend to help his dad at the fairs. Now this boy is smart as a whip. The other day . . . ah, here we are . . . The other day he won a competition at school. . . . No, no, only what's on the meter, not a cent more. . . . That's my way. There are guys at the rank who charge increments—fifty percent extra if the passenger's a foreigner, twenty percent if they figure he's from out of town . . . but for me there's a name for that: dishonesty. I charge what the meter reads. . . . But, just to finish, this kid, my grandson, João Paulo, he won a math competition, would you believe it? Say, let me give you my card, it's got my cell phone number on it; if you need a cab, just give me a buzz: Claudinor, look no more. Much obliged, chief, safe journey. See you when you get back!

42. List (2)

ALONE—White man, 34, 5ft 5, 137 lbs, black hair, brown eyes, retailer. Looking for a white girl, short, affectionate, no addictions.

ANA KAZUE—40, would like to find a kind husband.

CLAUDINEI—Mulatto, 33, 5ft 7, 163 lbs, brown eyes and hair. Driver. Wants to correspond with a blonde, aged 18 to 30,

interested in a serious relationship. Would like a letter with photo or phone number.
GERMAN—46, 5ft 10, 123 lbs, blond hair, blue eyes, white. Retiree, likes to travel. Wants to correspond with mulatto women.
IVONETE—White, 22, 5ft 8, 150 lbs, brown eyes and hair. Nutrition technician, smoker, sincere and affectionate. Wants to correspond with single men over 25.
LILLIAN—White, 19, 5ft 2, 105 lbs, brown eyes and hair. Student, Pisces, sweet and affectionate. Would like to correspond with men aged 19 to 25, white, water signs (Pisces, Cancer, Scorpio).
MARIA APARECIDA—Dark-skinned, 28, 5ft 9, 147 lbs, brown eyes and hair. Secretary, single, no children, loves to read. Likes paintings, good conversation and travel. Would like to meet cultured men, aged 30 to 40, over 5ft 9, single or divorced, well-resolved and honest. Preferably European.
MULATTO WOMAN—Beautiful, sweet, delicate. Third-level education. Art lover, looking for a woman with the same characteristics to hang out with, no strings attached.
NEAR-PERFECT LOVE—If you believe that we are nothing without the gaze—the love—of another . . . Looking for someone under 30, more or less. 5ft 8, 165 lbs. not a player, masculine, nonsmoker, good social level, handsome. Me, mature, special.
NEIDE NASCIMENTO—White, 39, 5ft 3, 128 lbs, brown eyes and hair. Administrative technician and primary school teacher. Likes objective people. Would like to correspond with men of 35 or over with a good head, sort of old-school.
NEREU PINTO DA SILVA—Black, 40, 5ft 3, 110lbs, black hair and eyes. Liberal, esoteric author. Wants to correspond with a woman of a good social and cultural level.

NESTOR—White, 67, 5ft 11, 185lbs, brown hair and eyes. Social worker. Would like to correspond with people of either sex throughout Brazil who like a range of subjects, travel, social work, newspapers, magazines, and videos.
NISSEI—Third-level graduate, happy-go-lucky, looking for you, thin, beautiful, independent, established.
RAIMUNDO N.S.—Pale-skinned mulatto, 35, 5ft 8, 176 lbs, brown hair and eyes. Works in graphics. Simple, caring, and romantic. Would like to correspond with women aged 25 to 35 who are affectionate and romantic.
WALESKA—Seeks friendship only.

43. Gaavá (pride)

It's red now. It's been purple, orange, crimson, and occasionally even of indeterminate color, but pretty much always dyed. And she, beautiful, as ever. A tribal tattoo on the small of her back, almost down to her coccyx; the left nostril delicately pierced with a discreet diamond stud, accentuating her perfect nose; Fanny is her name. She comes off as a teenage Madonna—salacious innocence, angelic debauchery. She's the brain and the voice of a garage band, the Naked Snake, a name suggested by her father, Bernardo, a quantity surveyor, Beatlemaniac (member of the Revolution fan club), a voracious reader of the "sublime tradition" of Judaic-American literature (Norman Mailer, Bernard Malamud, Saul Bellow, Philip Roth, Isaac Bashevis Singer, J. D. Salinger). When he was young, he dreamed of chucking it all in and hitting the road, taking hundreds of hysterical girls on a tour of social clubs in hinterland towns, with his long hair, psychedelic clothes, marijuana, LSD, who knows maybe cut a record or two, make the charts, become famous, get rich. . . . However, at university he got involved in student politics, and then, in the USA, specialized in surveying for large-scale structures. He got married, separated, then divorced.

Fanny writes all the band's songs. She gets home from school, has lunch, takes a shower, then locks herself into her room, where the hours slug their way across the walls, the rays of sun glance across the tree boughs of Higienópolis Avenue, the solitude of a cigarette burning down in an ashtray, the diet coke can sweating on the wooden floor, the bar of chocolate melting on the messed-up bed, and the guitar nesting comfortably in her arms, the manicured fingernails strumming out the chords, *blem-blom, blem-blom,* her vacant stare roaming a hall of mirrors, forking gardens, flooded corridors, her long, elegant fingers jotting down verses, in English, which fall like leaves onto the virgin pages of a spiral notebook. Afterwards, she'll head to her father's studio, where they'll convert the stock ESL phrases into the hip street talk of San Francisco and New York, into the no-holds-barred vernacular of her trash and grunge CDs—to the absolute horror of her Sunday-school mother, Raquel, a linguistic "purist."

Her parents encourage her, each in their own way. Even when she was a small kid, Bernardo used to set up a little stage for her at the party house on Bahia Street, where, with the help of a sophisticated karaoke machine smuggled in from Miami, Fanny would perform her best imitations of her idols. A real blast! Three years ago, for her bat mitzvah, she stamped her feet until her parents agreed to trade in the formal do at the Hebraica for a debut gig by her band at a bar in Paraíso, with her father's enthusiastic support and a resigned sigh from her mother. Raquel always reminded Bernardo that, seeing as they lived separately, it was she who had to adopt the bad-cop role, always on Fanny's back about school, tests, friends, going through her bag for drugs or condoms, rifling her wardrobe in search of a diary that could indicate how she was negotiating the ways of the world. . . . That's tiring, she'd say. Bernardo listens attentively, then says, Raquel, don't you think it's time Fanny cut a demo? Ah, go to hell, Bernardo, and she turns on her heel and leaves him standing there. There's a studio in Vila Madalena, if they rehearsed real hard, got everything down to a T, hmm, he ponders, scratching his beard.

Fanny is an artist. She's a great guitar player, a respectable drummer, she can play any tune by ear, and she's spellbinding on stage: the knee-high black boots running onto the light blond down of her shapely thighs, the black leather miniskirt hinting at the venus callipyge underneath, the black wings of her blouse tapering into lascivious claws, her mane, now red, falling wildly about her shoulders, her rasping, janisjoplin voice. Bernardo is thinking about chucking it all in, devoting himself full time to managing his daughter's career. Testing, testing! One, two! One, two! Hello, hello! Testing, testing! One, two! One, two! Testing!

44. Work

Every day at five in the afternoon he heads for home, in Boi Malhado, on foot, because he doesn't have the bus fare. He's taken a ton of courses, at job centers, training centers for the unemployed, workers' centers, but none of them paved the way to a new job. It was all just pretext for consensual slavery, eight hours of slog for a pittance at the end of the month, but hey, it's better than sitting on his butt all day, at least he's getting paid rather than paying. So he makes his way back to his father-in-law's place, where he's spent the last three years crammed into a tiny room with a double bed, dressing table, wardrobe, baby's crib, packed in like sardines, but they're not living off anybody, no siree, they have their pride. The wife drives a school van her father started running, not an official one, of course, couldn't afford to go legit—first they'd have to pull in more cash, then there's the government's share—but the schools are supportive and it brings in enough to tide them over. Things went sour last week, cuz the youngest, still single, said she's got a bun in the oven. The father-in-law blew his top, said his job was to bring up his own, not his grandkids, but the mother-in-law said that no flesh of her flesh was gonna be kicked out into the streets, and that was that. The real whipping boy is the son-in-law, the butt of all the jokes, abased in front of the whole neighborhood. What used to be whispers, jeers, and hehehes behind closed doors is now out-and-open mockery, not even the mongrel sniffs him anymore, the bum. And now he's really hit rock bottom: after a good grilling, the wife found out that he's in debt to pretty much everybody—the bar, the bakery, the convenience store, the supermarket, paltry tabs, nothing to shout about, but, women! now she controls every single cent, to the point that they have breakfast late so as to cut down on lunch, and he heads to the city center, on foot, to buy cigarettes, because the stomach can do without, and walking is good for circulation, but renege on his cigs is out of the question, he'd be nervy enough he could kill. On Sundays, when the brothers-and-sisters-in-law, the husbands and wives and kids come over early in the morning, when he's just waking up, he sneaks to his wife's handbag and swipes whatever spare change he can find and slips out, to idle away the day in Ibirapuera Park, lying on the grass, watching the water-jet fountain in front of the House of Assembly, watching the clouds form and dissolve, wishing the day would cave in and everything would just

45. Partial view of the city

são paulo streaks of lightning
(is são paulo the out-there? is it the in-here?)

on foot the landscape deflates

The old woman sits at the window
face wrinkles nylon handbag slumped on her lap inside things wrapped in newspaper white dress with black polka dot plastic sandals torture bunions gray hair frightened eyes she'll never get used to the traffic the rush the noise *the rope sings in the pulley the bucket brings up some briny water the silence the cows mooing the dry crust crumbles between the toes*

teenage girl in the aisle seat

dozes off teetering pile of matriculation prep binders spills from her arms, some going window-side onto the old lady who takes a start so sorry

(straightens up shifts aisleward)

She tries but it's impossible to keep her eyes open awake since early part-time shift at the counter of a travel agency then matriculation prep in the afternoons and an hour-and-a-half bus ride home where her mother looks at her and asks honey is it really worth it?

and crumbs from her dreams spill onto the old woman's shoulder

standing just behind a man with one hand on his bag strap the other hand in his pocket (uniform, lunch box, toothbrush, toothpaste, comb, comic book) lets his bulk sway his eyes half closed (half open?) tired sweating bills to pay installments in arrears his bulk

forward

and

back

another Fierabras with few friends
tries to figure where's he's at
crouches to look between arms and armpits
tries to recognize someplace
neophyte
we sleep we snore until
we reach our stop and a bell rings
inside the head and we reach to ring the bell

rattling down Rebouças Avenue
the traffic light shifts green to red
cars and cars

bums peddlers boys girls
cars and cars
thieves muggers hookers dealers
cars and cars
another day
tuesday
weekend far away
the streetlights headlights lights on the electronic panels of the buses
and everything is the color of tiredness
and the bodies are even more tired
more tired
my calves are killing me my head is killing me my

46. The mayor does not like anyone looking him in the eye

We were told as much right on the first day. Doctor Abdala, master of ceremonies, gathered the kitchen staff together and said, Now there'll be no persecution, none, I assure you. "He" (when Doctor Abdala says "He" he immediately glances skyward, as if the mayor were looking down upon us) "He" knows that not all of you voted for him, but so what? What matters here is the work! And the best that each of you has to offer. So do not worry, nobody will be forced out. Those who do not fit our needs will be transferred, no more than that. Personable, he continued with his pep talk, calling us "colleague," slapping us on the shoulder, explaining the minutiae of what "He" planned to do for the city, canvassing when none was necessary, the man was already elected, after all, but he said that the mayor was a nice guy, that he was going to put an end to all the thieving, that his administration would focus on the needy, and that the mayor and the staff at city hall were one and the same, and then he began to list the mayor's likes and dislikes: his coffee has to be piping hot, never reheated, "Never! Understood?" with five drops of Assugrin sweetener, don't forget that, "He is terrified of getting fat!"; sometimes "He" gets a migraine, so bring two aspirin and a glass of fresh water, "Pay attention, I said fresh, not chilled, fresh!"; lunchtime is sacred, one thirty on the button, not a minute more, or he flies into a rage; dessert is a slice of chilled pineapple cut into six equal sections, "Understood? Six equal sections. Measure them if need be, but they must be rigorously equal!" and accompanied by a single napkin, "One!" One fork, one knife. On doctor's orders, due to a gastric problem, "He" takes afternoon tea at half-past four, a ranitidine with a glass of water. . . . "Fresh! That's right," and a cream cracker with a cup of tea, "But, for the love of God, never serve black tea! Understand? Black tea is out! National herbal teas, particularly fennel, will do nicely." When "He" has to stay late in his cabinet, he has to nibble something before dinner, which is never taken before half-past nine, but you needn't worry about that, as generally he dines at a restaurant, what with decisions still to be made, themes to discuss, and so on; "the mayor's middle name is 'work.' " "He" is the sort that likes everything just so, black and white, "So, my friends . . . my colleagues, no standing about gossiping in the hallways! Down to work! To work!" That's what makes these allegations so ludicrous, this spurious gossip that "He" has offshore bank accounts, that "He" bought a triplex apartment in Jardins, that "He" is the boss of the crime ring that has robbed the city blind. . . . For me, "He" is just like any of the others who have held this post. And his wife, Janice, is such a sweet person. She came here once to see how her husband was being treated and she was greatly impressed, and told me so. At the time, Vaguinho, my godson, was out of work, so I said, Milady, if I may, do you think it might be possible to arrange a post for my godson, Vaguinho, a fine lad, hardworking, though he can't seem to find a placement, I believe on account of his not finishing secondary education, and she said, We shall see, and told her aide to write down my name and request. Time went by, and I was giving up hope, when I received a phone call from the chief of staff for the regional administration of Campo Limpo telling me that Vaguinho was to turn up for work the following day, employment book in hand. He is now happy as Larry, enjoying the respect of one and all: his job is to lead people to and from the mayor's appearances, where they are to clap and cheer and, on his signal, chant the mayor's name, and triumphantly carry him aloft in return for free sandwiches a cold drink and a few bucks, the sum varies depending on the importance of the event. Vaguinho is something of a bodyguard and has, on several occasions, been at very close quarters with the man himself, and he can confirm, resolutely, that it is expressly and utterly forbidden for anyone to look the mayor in the eye.

47. "Cranium"

up in the community cranium is the freakiest of dudes but that's what makes him the best liked
he's sixteen nearly five foot eleven
[goin' on 200 pounds

black like the water that runs between the shanties
his teeth are white and fine like no one else's
and most of all he's my brother
though I'm dark chocolate goin' on mulatto, short and
[missing teeth
and there was another brother who was pale sarará
that was his nickname even, sarará
but he bought it on a bad lay when still
[a minor
see our momma hooked up lots but took no crap
from sons-uv-bitches wantin' to beat on her ass
hardworkin', she kept her own wolf from the door
never needed no man, our momma
and they were all smoked anyway, by the pigs
the goons or some dumbass overdose

but cranium my brother doesn't smoke or blow

he spends the whole day reading and eating which he says are his
[vices
He reads or eats everything he can get his hands on
He's got this old shoebox he takes out sometimes
cleaning fluid razors dusters glue cardboard
and he'll take any old beat-up book
coverless dog-eared ripped up half dead
and he'll fix that up good as new
like some doctor at the ER
he's bangin', he's the man
I like him not because he's my bro

the whole hood gives him respect
the mommas all point him out as an example
whenever I see him lookin' mopey
sprawled out on his bed with nothin' to do
I go out there and find some way to pick me up a book
but a thick-ass book, the thicker the better, cuz he says
thin books can't stand up worth a damn

they're favela-books, he jokes, don't even deserve to live
when cranium laughs it's like the place lights up around him
them good white teeth like headlights in the dark

once we braced a postman and took him to some waste
[land
we slit up that sack and spilled its gut out on the floor of some
[abandoned house
we started pickin' out checkbooks and credit cards
and feeling up them envelopes all airmail par avion
cuz there's always some dumbass who sends cash in the mail
then I came across these pudgy brown envelopes
with string wrapped around a clasp
and I asks the postman-dick if they be books
and he nods a yes
so I stuck them under my arm and we zipped
I sent a dude over to cranium with the books but no
[envelopes
because my li'l bro is systematic like that
he'd never open no mail that weren't addressed to him
then when I came home three days later

he bearhugs me and says jeez man way cool
and starts praising the books one by one, by name
but he liked one the most, genius he said
and he grabbed that big thick book, spartacus I think
[by howard fast
the cranium was thrilled to bits and I was proud
to have a brother so intelligent
who's got a notebook where he notes the title and the author
when he got the book when he started reading it and when he finished
with comments on every one in that tiny handwriting of his
when he's reading cranium looks like a buddha
sometimes I invite him to go sink some beers with the guys
at a clean club or bar over in campo belo
and he gets to tellin' us we're a bunch of suckers
stickin' our necks out sellin' blow with the cops breathin' down
[our necks
you're the ones who get smoked he says
and the playboy in his mansion in morumbi
who's the real boss behind the business
he's gettin' richer and richer, his kids off studying abroad
bulletproof imported car with bodyguards
butler nanny gardener kitchen staff housekeeping
the johns in his pocket
and we're up here like flies on shit
waiting to get clipped like ants queuing outside an anthill
waiting for the grim reaper
and the crew get all shirty

but no one says nothin' because they know deepdown the cranium's right
he's always right
and cranium got mad as hell when he found out that we whacked a vic
who tried to fight back
a shaky-handed amateur got scared and pop he ghosts the guy at the lights
and cranium says you dumbfucks the rich aren't down in the streets
they're up there in their choppers
pissin' themselves laughin' at me and you hustlin' down here
cranium was fumin'
for him, what we should be doin' is stockin' them guns for a revolution
he only agrees with bank jobs and armored car heists
kidnappin' some millionaire, or occupyin' land or abandoned houses

cranium is deep

when he turned fifteen
we put two butt-naked hoochies in his bed
we went out drinkin', even lit some candles, really takin' the piss
and when he came back, kinda baked
he flopped into bed without turnin' on the lights
and jumped back up when he saw the naked hos, man, hand-picked by a pimp
top-dollar booty, we even had to pass a hat to raise the cash

but cranium wasn't havin' it, he got himself dressed and zipped
so he calls me out and starts raggin' on me
and I was so toasted all I could do was laugh
he got madder and madder then huffs off down an alley
anyone else and I'd a clipped him
a real situation, the gals found it kinda weird
but cranium was right
he said that whenever he wanted some ass he didn't need our help
[in gettin' it
cranium's like that

he's a romantic
he fessed up one day that he writes poetry
I'll show you someday he says
I said he should lend the notebooks to the rap crew
I know some people who could put it to music
and he says no my poetry's to be read not rapped
and he started reciting some verses from a book riquinho
[found in the street
it was complicated shit and I didn't understand a fuckin'
[thing
but I said I liked it and he laughed pretending he believed me
and I said man cranium's bitchin'

the other day cranium was stopped at the mouth of the favela
the MPs were trollin'
they demanded ID
but he ain't got no social security no employment book
so they made him lie facedown in the dirt

his mug almost in the stream of runnin' sewage
they cuffed his arms and legs and left him there
humiliated, and the whole community was up in revolt
so they threw him in the back of the pig wagon and zipped
driving him round são paulo, end to end,
beatin' on him, torturin' his ass
and cranium was fucked up, cranium
who's got no beef with no man
but that's aight, cuz we hustled this fink into comin' across
with the names addresses shifts of the pigs who done over
my brother and tonight's gonna be a long night
so I'm goin' to pick up my Glock over with cranium
cuz he keeps our roscoes and shells in his box of books
and he always asks me what the need is and I'm gonna have to lie
because cranium would never agree with what we're about to do

that's the problem with cranium right there, man, he's got a heart
[this damn big

48. The Minuano

the girl treaded softly on the frozen dewy ground in her new leather sandals, her feet sheathed in gray socks, with holes in the toes, her schoolbag heavy with notebooks filled with careful handwriting the Italian headmistress butch but excellent always patted the girl on the head and she jumps aboard the noisy tractor-drawn carriage with all the other schoolgirls and they chug off toward the country schoolhouse, rattling and gigging and shaking with the cold and bucking around like goats laughing their heads off it was june and the sky was blue blue blue and the girl was all chuffed with her jet-black braids and her pooly-blue eyes looked across the soya plantations and she was happy because her father was in the fields with his two older brothers and this year he said the harvest would be good when they gathered in the evening round the wood stove heating water for chimarrão tea and her baby brother growing by the day so pretty soon he'll be out running around in the yard hooting and howling being heard way off in the fields by three tiny dots her dad and his brothers with hats on their heads and her mother in the kitchen cooking chicken in sauce with manioc and she swaying this way and that way in the back of the truck her radiant blue eyes scanning the green expanse of rolling hills and she was so happy the kind of happiness we feel at seven years of age and which now, with the stereo pounding on the thirteenth floor of an apartment high-rise in cerqueira césar, as she's spread out drunk on the floor, she desperately recognizes my god how did I let it crumble and slip between my fingers where did I lose it when my god when

49. Tuesday ritual, the Moon in Cancer

In a corner of the living room, erect a small altar and adorn it with flowers. In the middle, place a plate with seeds and herbs and add a pink crystal. Light a pink candle and some rose-scented incense. Fetch an unused cloth of any color, spread it on the altar and sprinkle seeds and herbs whilst offering each to the goddess of the Moon, beseeching domestic peace and marital bliss. Close the bag, tie the mouth, and carry it with you. Give thanks.

50. A letter

Guidoval, May 2, 2000

Dear Paulino, my son,

I'm writing these brief lines just to send you our news and to ask word of you and the family. All is good here. Your father is laid up at the moment because he stubbed his foot on a stump covered over by brushwood. You know how stubborn your father can be. He flatly refused to stop by the hospital and his foot took to swelling. It almost left him with tetanus. So, against his will, he went to the doctor, with his foot swelled up like a football and red as I've never seen the like. . . .

And you, son, have you been eating properly? Just yesterday I met Zé Gomes, remember him? The one who lives out in Zezim Francisco, he's got a shop running now, swanky stuff, and he was asking after you. He said you used to play ball together on the pitch in Zezim Francisco. He reckons you may have dated his sister Sueli at some stage. She's married now and lives in Ponte Nova.

Has it been cold there lately? It's getting chilly at night here now, so you need a blanket. You remember how I take ill this time of year, nearly dying a death? Well, nothing's changed there. When afternoon falls and that yellow dust starts to swirl my nose gets bunged up, I get short of breath, it's suffocating, I feel like each is my last, son, I wouldn't wish it on my worst enemy. Have you been wrapping up warm? The doctor says I have to use an inhaler, but where am I going to get the money for one of those? They cost an eye.

And how is Marcia? And the kids? Gislaine must be huge by now. The last time I saw her was three years ago and she was already a lass. How time flies. I can only imagine the size of her now. And Maico? Is that how you spell his name? Pardon me, son, but it's a difficult name. . . . Pretty, but difficult. And Juninho? Aren't you ever going to bring them over to see us, son? Your father has grown so old. God forgive me, but someday soon he won't be with us anymore, Paulino. You never know, do you? And he'd dearly love to see the grandkids just one more time. Talk to Marcia. If you explain it to her I'm sure she'll understand. She's a mother too.

I was almost forgetting. Adélia is engaged to be married in September. Why don't you take the opportunity? Tiãozinho finally got some sense. He went halves on a truck with his father and does removals for the Parmas over in Ubá. Adélia is thrilled. Think about it, won't you, son?

Sometimes when I turn in for the night I think about you, my son, who I carried inside me, who's been through so much in this life, and I just can't accept this misunderstanding, this distance. I feel this knot in my chest, it's a strange sensation. I know it's just a mother thing, and I don't mean to bother you. You don't deserve that.

Poor Silky is so old now. He's blind in the left eye, which keeps running all the time. He can hardly waddle along after us anymore. He just lies there, in a corner of the yard, near the mango tree, sleeping, and we have to bring him food and water. That's age. It'll happen to us all someday.

Well, Paulino, I have so much to say to you, but I don't want to take up more of your time.

Everyone sends their love, to you, Marcia, and the kids.

And a special kiss for you, dear son. Think about what I said.

Your father told me to say that he prays for you every day at seven o'clock mass and that you're not to worry, because the Infant Jesus will be forever by your side.

A kiss for a dear son from a mother who misses him.
I love you
Glorinha

51. Politics

I can't turn him down, see? he's very well known, he's always in the newspapers, on TV, he's from the countryside, has a mountain of money, he's in the coffee business I think. He sends me to pick up his car on Thursdays, his personal car, the Pajero, not the official car, from the Legislature, and I drive over to a house in Moema, I won't give the address, because it could cause problems, but it's a decent place, with no name on the façade or anything, just walking by you'd never suspect anything, so then I pick up three girls, the prime sort, university students only, I know because I pay them, I stop by the bank, take out the money and pay them in cash, the old man's no fool, he's going on seventy, but he's no fool, one time I brought him a girl who was on the cover of *Sexy* magazine, you might know who I mean, the congressman saw the cover and said this one frequents the house, make sure you bring her, so I did, man, you had to see this chick! So I take them over to a hotel on Alameda Santos, I won't say the name, could cause me problems, the congressman is a well-known figure, I don't want any trouble! it's always the little fish who takes the fall, and that means me, so I leave the girls at the hotel and head for Vila Madalena, where I know this fag who pimps some guys, never the same guys, so I hire three of them and take them by car to the hotel too, calling the cocaine delivery guy on the way, who drops off the blow, discreetly, but it's not for the congressman, he's against drugs, of course this service is more expensive, but he says money's not an issue, and in the meantime I get his whiskey, just the good stuff, scotch, because the congressman has no patience for Jack Daniel's or shit like that, which is American, and he hates the Americans, the cocaine is for the guys and the dolls, but the congressman doesn't force anything on anyone, you snort if you want, I get the whiskey from a friend of mine who brings it in from Paraguay, so it's cheaper, first-rate stuff too, eighteen years old, blue label, I even had to score some marijuana once, for a girl who said she didn't do coke or alcohol, but liked to smoke a joint beforehand, to calm her nerves, because she didn't like turning tricks, said she only did it because she had to, to pay her college fees, but then they all say that, don't they? I mean, not all, some of them do it because they like it, I know some who, just to look at them, you know they're in it for the sex, well, so

I show them to the presidential suite (the manager knows the score), leave them to chill a little, and I go check the ashtrays, the congressman hates tobacco, but since everyone in this line smokes he tolerates it, then I make sure the glasses are all clean, the towels too, the congressman trusts no one, only me, and then he comes out and sits naked in an armchair, whiskey tumbler in hand, and I leave, locking the door behind me, and go down to the bar to talk to the barman, who's a friend of mine, and he always speculates about what sort of shit they get up to in there, but I just say that I don't know and don't want to know, because it's none of my business, and then we hang there talking, mostly about politics, because it's a subject I like, and him too.

52. In white

Shoulders slumped, Dr. Fernando sat down on the edge of the lower bunk, kicked off his white shoes and slid them under the bed, stretched his white-stockinged toes one by one, with relish, reached out for the remote control abandoned on a chair, turned on the TV, sound muted, and flicked through the channels to the evening news, then laid his muscles and bones upon the thin slab of foam that served as a mattress. He liked lying there like that, eyes half open, divining the bombardment of colors, the day splayed across the yellow walls of the dorm. From his consultancy to the hospital, twenty kilometers of rucked asphalt, exhaust fumes from panicked engines and stereotypical drivers. His cell phone rings in three bursts of peal. The first, Claudia, Do you remember where you left the receipt for Ju's ballet classes? I'm mad late, do you remember where you left it? What do you mean *no*? I gave you the bill to pay. Oh forget it! It's always the same, you never know anything! The second, Ligia, Hi . . . Where are you? Wow! (inaudible) . . . duty? That's a pity! Listen, one of these days we should (inaudible) . . . There's a bar over on (inaudible) . . . Kisses . . . See ya. . . . The third, Claudia, What's (inaudible) . . . to you? Well? Can you hear me? I found you (inaudible) . . . strange . . . Are you sure? (inaudible) . . . happened? Can you hear me? Tomorrow (inaudible) . . . to (inaudible) . . . a mother's day gift. Hello? Hell-o? A night born calmly: some unimportant stitches, one alcoholic coma, an allergic reaction, no "killer washboards," stabbed drunks, hit-and-run victims, injuries from street fights or car crashes. Lead eyelids seal his orbs, never enough sleep, too much stress, from duty doctor to the consultancy, consultancy back to the hospital, accumulated functions, vacations? How long has *that* been?

a house they rented in Barra do Sahy, the soles of his feet sinking in the dark brown sands of Baleia Beach, the late afternoon, Ju's wobbly little legs running ahead

he woke up with a start, the bell wailing, "Dr. Fernando! Dr. Fernando! Emergency! Emergency!" The fine white socks locate his white shoes, the TV flatlines, his fingers pat down his thinning hair, he throws open the door, "Mario! Hey, Mario!" "Dr. Fernando, how are the batteries holding up?" "Fit as a fiddle. What do you know about this emergency?" "Looks like a punk got some daylight put in him." "A fight?" "Don't think so . . . A robbery . . ." "Is he the perp or the vic?" "Don't know, the cops brought him in," so they made their way through the maze of patients and relatives jamming up the corridors. In the surgical center he donned his mask and greens, sterilized his hands, tied up his apron, snapped on the surgical gloves, nodded at the anesthesiologist, Dr. Tarciso, caught a glimpse of the resident, Jorge? Isn't that his name, Jorge? ah! the SA, Sonia, gorgeous! Ah, Sonia, when are we going to meet up for a quick fuck? he asks in thought, Jorge (yeah, Jorge, that's his name) informed him that the bullet entered through the stomach and lodged in the lung, causing major hemorrhaging, Right, so let's get to it. Approaching the table, the monitor connected, irregular heartbeat, the flash of recognition, what the fuck!

Claudia kicking and screaming, pulling at her hair, eyes wild

Ju whimpering with a revolver to her nape

make her shut the fuck up or I'll

Claudia for the love of God tell him where the dollars are

—Tarciso, cancel the anesthetic. . . .

—What?

—Cancel it, it's not worth it. . . .

—What do you mean "it's not worth it"?

—He's in critical condition, Dr. Fernando, but I

(interrupting the resident)

—Shut up (he doesn't bother with his name)

Dr. Fernando pulled off his mask and stepped away from the surgical table, shouting loudly, he turned back:

—Tarciso . . . you remember the break-in? The break-in at my house? Yeah, well, this is the guy. . . . He was one of them! I'm not gonna save him, no way! I'm not gonna lift a finger to save this guy. . . . He nearly ruined my life, he almost fucked everything up. . . . I'm not gonna operate on him, you hear me? You can call someone else in, you can report me to the RMC, do whatever you like, I don't care, I don't give a damn, you hear? I don't care.

And he disappeared behind the glass doors of the theater.

The anesthesiologist stood there in silence.

The SA stared blankly, hypnotized by the clock on the wall.

The resident monitored the patient's heartbeat, as his breathing turned convulsive

53. Tetralogue

A: Good evening

M: Good evening

R: Good evening

N: Good evening

A: Is this . . . your first . . . time?

R: Yes . . .

A: Well, so . . . erm . . . well . . . My name is Arnaldo, I'm an engineer, partner in a construction firm . . . a small one . . . this is Monica . . . my wife.

R: It's a pleasure.

N: Nice to meet you.

M: I'm . . . a pediatrician. . . .

R: Right, a pediatrician? Well . . . it's . . . it's a little . . . awkward . . . for us, I guess. . . . My name . . . I'm Rafael . . . an economist . . . university lecturer . . . and this is my . . . my wife. . . . She's a designer. . . .

A: Designer?

N: Yeah, I work with . . . ah, Rafael forgot to say . . . my name's Nancy.

A: Ah, Nancy!

N: Yeah . . . I work with jewelry. . . . I have a small company. . . .

A: A small-business owner, right. . . .
R: Yeah, like I said to her . . . if she'd kept the business under the radar, like before, she'd earn a lot more . . . now, the turnover barely pays the taxes . . . the government takes most of it. . . .
M: That's the truth. . . . In my case . . . at the surgery . . . I don't give receipts. If the client insists I say, okay, but it's twenty percent extra. . . . The clients usually . . . understand. . . .
N: Yeah, but I had to go official, because I wanted to sell my jewelry in shopping malls . . . an opportunity came up. . . . Now I've got this export contract. . . .
M: Export?
N: Just small volumes to start with . . . to France . . . But who knows?
M: I'd love to see your work!
A: I must confess, we have to operate with high working capital, so you can keep a lot of that off the books. . . . If we didn't, and I hate to say it, but if we didn't, we wouldn't be able to complete the projects . . . basically it's the money off the books that keeps the company running. . . . The workers have to be paid on time . . . and there's the security equipment too . . . and there are always payment delays . . . so we have to have that margin to work with. . . . Imagine if we closed down? How many northeasterners would be out of work and in the streets . . .
M: Yeah, and robbing us at the traffic lights . . .
N: Exactly . . . and we're not even safe in our own homes. . . .
A: Right . . . so you live in a house?
N: No, in an apartment . . .

A: You're lucky. . . . We live in a house. . . . It's dangerous as hell. . . . You have to have security . . . which is an added cost that we shouldn't have to shoulder. . . . I mean, we pay our taxes. . . .
M: You have to have a security car doing the rounds, all night long. . . . Any problem, they can take care of it . . . Once I stopped in front of the garage, I was listening to a CD I really like, the Carpenters, so I stopped there awhile just to hear out a song. . . . In moments there was this car behind me, sirens flashing. . . .
R: You know, we, the middle class, we're basically under siege. . . .
N: Exactly right . . .
A: Under siege!
M: That's it exactly. . . .
A: Well, I think we can already consider ourselves friends, right?
N: Yes, right.
M: So, shall we . . . get down . . . to business?
R: Er . . . Arnaldo . . . Monica . . . Would you mind if we . . . Nancy and I . . . took a moment . . . to talk it over . . . just the two of us . . . just to be . . .
A: Sure, sure . . .
M: Of course . . . we'll just pop over to the bar . . . for a drink. . . .
(*pause*)
R: So . . . what do you think?
N: I dunno. . . .
R: Do you want to go through with this . . . this . . .
N: Fantasy . . .
R: Fantasy?
N: Well . . . I think . . . I think it could be good . . . for our relationship. . . . I don't know. . . . That's what I think. . . .
R: Did you like Arnaldo? That's if Arnaldo's his real name . . .

N: Sheez, Rafael, there you go with your paranoia again. The people that come here are decent people . . . civilized. . . . Didn't you see? The guy's a businessman . . . the wife's a doctor. . . .

R: Yeah . . . I don't know. . . .

N: Are you going to start? If you don't want to do it we'll leave right now . . . say sorry, but it's a no-go. . . .

R: Me? Back out? Now? No . . . Bottle blonde . . . she's a bottle blonde, isn't she?

N: Monica? Yeah, she dyes her hair. . . . But she's pretty . . . attractive. . . .

R: She's attractive all right.

N: See? Admit it . . . you liked her, am I right?

R: Nancy, don't be silly, you know you're the only woman for me. . . . I only came here because you insisted. . . .

N: If you want to leave we'll leave . . . like I said. . . . And cut the cynicism, okay . . . I know you . . . you can't fool me. . . .

R: For me . . .

N: Monica's not bad, but the husband . . .

R: What's wrong with the husband?

N: He's a bit old, isn't he?

R: Yeah, a bit . . . Not a patch on me . . . right?

N: No comparison . . .

R: Right, so . . .

N: Well . . . tell him . . . it's on. . . .

R: Okay, so wait here while I go settle the . . . close the . . . busi . . . I mean the . . . the . . .

54. Diploma

**Church of the Quadrangular Gospel
National Evangelic Crusade**

This is to certify that PAULO ROBERTO ERNESTI, born FEBRUARY 7, 1931, upon the profession of his faith in Our Lord Jesus Christ, was baptized in accordance with the teachings of the Word of God (Mark 16:15–16; Acts 2:38)

São Paulo MARCH 8, 1978

PASTOR NEEMIAS SANTORO DA SILVA
(officiating)

55. Online

I'm telling you, man, twenty-five! Twenty-five through the internet alone, the chat sites, the ICQs. And I don't bullshit anyone either, I say it straight from the start: I'm short, on the pudgy side, shortsighted . . . but very virile! No Viagra needed! I'll do anything in bed. . . . So then I throw out some poetry. Vinicius de Moraes is fail-safe. But sometimes you gotta resort to cheap tricks, so I bought the collected works of J. G. de Araújo Jorge at a second-hand bookstore. . . . And if the chick is more . . . say . . . intellectual, I go for Byron! You know . . . the usual stuff . . . All a woman really wants is a good fuck with someone affectionate, romantic. . . . But not gay! These days, if a guy's a romantic, he's gay; if he's macho, he's insensitive, a troglodyte. . . . I blend the two: I'm a macho romantic. . . . I've restored the word as an instrument of seduction, understand? The melody of verse nibbling at the earlobe . . . Man! I praise their beauty with borrowed lines. . . . Of course, they don't need to know that, but I figure even if they did, they'd still call. Poems are not written to languish on pages, but to become part of our collective memory. . . . So I draw on all the knowledge garnered as a myopic kid reading away in his room when the other boys were off playing ball. . . . There is a time when women want muscles, biceps, triceps, all that malarkey. . . . Then they discover that even a dog can fuck . . . and well at that, judging by the flicks you see out there. . . . So they start looking around for something more, you see? I make first contact on the chat sites, I introduce myself, and then you see pretty quick whether or not we're, say, soul mates. . . . If so, we exchange ICQs, e-mail addresses. Then come the jokes, the false misunderstandings, the double entendres, and it's all blah-blah-blah, he-he-he, goochy-goochy-goo, a real game, dude, it's fascinating, the best game in the world, because the prize, if you win, is a woman in your bed . . . gagging to do whatever you ask . . . anything! And, let me tell you, I can't complain . . . I've bedded a sixteen-year-old, a virgin, would you believe it? And a married woman, fifty-three, slender as hell, with an ass and tits to put a teenager to shame; I did a doctor and her secretary; I've shagged black chicks, white chicks, Jap chicks, southern blondes, northeastern mulattas, and even a Jewess. There've been times I couldn't get it up, once with this gorgeous woman from the country, but, shit, she stank of beer; I tried once, twice, three times, but my head was elsewhere, I mean the head of my cock, of course. So I said to her, fuck, this has never happened to me before! I've gone five times in one night (with a Japanese chick, lust personified). This one time I had to change my telephone number because this loon, Leticia, kept on calling me and sending a thousand e-mails a day; I've had to turn down three marriage proposals; I even had to pay for therapy to convince this one woman not to leave her husband; I've caught STDs too. Man, I could tell you so many stories you could write a book. Twenty-five, man, twenty-five! I had to jump ship a few times too, because the girls didn't fit their descriptions. And this one time I got fucked over. This guy passed himself off as a woman, and then, when I turned up for the date, I was jumped by three headbangers, and they kicked the crap out of me, broke my glasses. I had to take three days' medical leave (I said I'd been run over, couldn't get the license plates) . . . but what's a guy to do . . . I love pussy. . . . Well, man, it was good talking to you, but I gotta go; time to go online. Can you get this? Thanks, man, call me, yeah? Sorry, man, gotta go, you take care.

56. Slow motion

the half-empty beer can traced a rotating descending arc over a sea of heads coordinates set for impact upon Marlon's scalp, and he immediately craned his neck forty-five degrees to see where the fuck the projectile had come from among the thousands of possible hands of anxious supporters packed onto the terraces of Pacaembu Stadium for that Corinthians versus Rosario Central, last sixteen of the Libertadores da América, and who does he clamp his eyes on but the motherfucker who'd robbed his repair shop in Vila Guilherme just days before, the bastard, I'm gonna break his neck, and he saw the thieving runt's eyes disappear among the forest of necks that had packed out the stadium that night

PC was watching Corinthians attack down the flank, a cross floated dangerously into the six-yard box, who knows, a goal might come of it, when a half-empty beer can traced a rotating descending arc over his head and he followed its progress until final impact upon the head of some guy, who immediately craned his neck around forty-five degrees to see where the fuck the projectile had come from only to clamp his eyes dead on PC and start to nudge some guy standing beside him and PC started thinking, shit, maybe he thinks I . . . , so, out of caution, he sank among the forest of necks that had packed the stadium that night

Marlon nudged Baldy who nudged his pals—fuck, do you think I wouldn't recognize the son of a bitch?—and they spread out, scanning the terraces, and it didn't take long to find out where the thieving little bastard was hunkering down

Marlon reached him, fuming out the ears, and said

Remember me, dumbfuck?

, and at this very moment the crowd moaned loud as the ball scraped some paint off the Rosario crossbar.

Hey, Marlon, what are we gonna do with him?

, asked Baldy, and his boss, distracted by some promising midfield play, replied vaguely

We're going to ram a broom handle up his ass

The gang shuddered with excitement

Cool! Let's do it!

And Marlon

Hey, dickhead, just so you see I'm a nice guy, I'm gonna let you watch the rest of the game,

and turning back to his pals,

After the game we'll take him to some scrub and stick a broom handle in his ass.

PC was crawling hands on knees scared stiff through a forest of hairy legs, ordinary trouser legs, dirty Chinese sneakers, worn shoes, jaded flip-flops until a pair of legs barred the way and trapped his head in a vise, he wanted to yell but Corinthians attacked and the crowd *ooh*ed and *ah*ed and then a bunch of other legs came scurrying up on him and someone said something about ramming a broom handle up his ass, but he figured it was a joke, things were bad enough as they were, but when he said it again he realized he meant it and then he lost his interest in watching the rest of the game but these guys were fanatics and sat down to watch and PC took to trying to remember how it was you prayed so he could beg god for extra time, a penalty shoot-out, for some miracle, any miracle, oh my god.

57. Newark, Newark

Zé Geraldo, flutters in his gut, hands welded to the arms of the chair, feet glued to the floor, arm hairs on end, as the plane taxied on the runway—he had no idea Boeings were this uncomfortable. The tower ordered the plane to a halt. Turbine after turbine swirled into supersonic life, rippling metal muscles, then it hurtled furiously down the asphalt tongue and plowed into the pitchy depths of unknown night. Only then did he half open his eyes, in time to see the flicker of a shantytown down below, Guarulhos, igneous nocturnal São Paulo slipping away, ah, maybe for the last time, maybe, probably.

By his side, an enormous lard ass in a suit; on the aisle, a girl, foreign-looking, eyeshade on, earphones in. The man is starting a book, in English, shit! a shiver down the spine, on his definitive way to the United States and he can't even speak the language! What about customs? More questions? The consulate had been hell, having to answer stuff he'd never even dreamed of, just to get a visa. Now, at ten thousand feet, a shudder, any more questions? Rick . . . My god! What if he doesn't . . . What if he isn't there? How would he get to Newark? Yes, he has the address, and he did promise, don't worry, everything will work out just fine, but what if? an accident or something, you never know . . . destiny . . . The time difference . . . An hour behind . . . So . . . that means he'll be landing at . . . The weather . . . Cloudy, high of thirty-four degrees, low of fourteen. Thank god, Rick came good. At least! Intelligent! He was smart, he'd already taken a course in English at CCAA, so he could speak a bit. But he, never, nothing . . . damn language! Ah, but at least he could conjugate the verb to be: I am you are he she it is we are you are—again—they are. Every year at school, same-old same-old. Sitting on the edge of her desk, the teacher, so then, let's go over the verb to be, then it's thighs and back at the board, chalking it out.

There was a time when he desperately devoured *Speak Up* magazine, but what about the comprehension? What did he say? oh shit, what was that he said? and not even sleeping with a tape recorder whirring under his pillow was any help at all, none!

Rick was anticipative, Relax, man, you'll learn the hard way! Rick's a master. Three years in New York and he's all set, with a cool apartment, respectable salary as a hot-plate cook, a hot-plate cook, imagine that! His spare time and cash he uses to study the arts at night. In Brazil, eight or ten hours graft just about pays the rent and food. . . . Rick did right. Things weren't working out, so he left. Now, earning in dollars, everyone respects Rick. And in letters, phone calls, always saying to him, Come up here, come on up! We'll have a blast! Rick is a great guy, but, you know . . . Stop pussyfootin' around, José Geraldo! Man up, are you gonna whine over this shithole of a country? This people with no gumption, a swindling elite, corruption, politicking, shiftiness, scumbaggery, cuckoldry, debauchery . . . Ah no . . . enough! to hell with it. . . .

The suit-and-tie closed the book and his eyes, what was that he was reading?

58. Juggling

They say that in Italy a man can't see a woman on her own or he approaches her, full of chivalry, to see if there's anything she needs, if he can help at all; a woman just has to sit on a park bench and over they'll come, all solicitous, because that's just how they are, handsome, green-eyed, tanned, dark-haired, strong, tall, just look at the Italian football team, and they're so polite, they treat women with the utmost attention, and it doesn't matter if she's pretty or ugly, slim or fat, black or white, they want to be of assistance, to look after women, because they know that's what women need. Of course, I've never been to Italy, which is a distant country, over in Europe, but I was told all this by a gentleman I was with once, who picked me out of a book at the agency on São Carlos do Pinhal Street, and I was still a girl at the time, only sixteen, but with the body of a twenty-one-year-old and fake ID, I went to meet him in his room, and he told me to take a shower, gave me imported shampoo, English soap, French perfume, and then he took me to Iguatemi mall, where he told me to pick out a real nice dress, a lady's dress, and some lingerie and shoes, and then he paraded me about on his arm, over to Jacques & Janine, and we went back to his hotel with all these shopping bags with swanky brand names, and as I got changed, he spoke to me of Italy as he donned his Versace suit. We took a cab to a swanky do in Moema, with security at the door, red carpet in the entrance, and I've never seen so many important people in my life, the clothes! the smells! it was a dream, a fairy tale, there were politicians, people from TV, journalists, and he kept real close to me the whole time, introducing me to friends and acquaintances, Patricia, this is so-and-so, Patricia, please meet . . . I don't know why he chose to call me Patricia, but whenever we were alone he'd whisper in my ear, you're beautiful, my god you're so beautiful, and I started to believe it, feeling, if only for a moment, like I was the loveliest woman in the world, and then, at a certain point, we left, and he took me to a restaurant in Jardins, a place I walked past once with a friend just so I could tell her I'd eaten there, though she didn't believe me, but I remember it to this day, Antiquarius is the name, on Oscar Freire, seriously chic and ultra-expensive, and he sat us down and ordered this cod dish, which was divine, and a bottle of wine, wow! the wine, but we drank only moderately, because that's one thing he did ask me from the beginning, not to drink too much, just accompany him, and then, as we ate some lupine seeds, he laid his hand on mine and said, looking me in the eye, pretend you're my wife, that you love me, that I'm the most important thing in the world to you, which wasn't hard to do because he was so sweet, so nice, and we spent the whole dinner that way, like father and daughter, or husband and wife, but never as if he were paying me to be there. Out on the sidewalk after dinner he asked me where I wanted to be taken, and I was surprised, and I said, why? don't you want to fuck me, of course I couldn't quite use those terms, but he understood, and he said to me, eyes downcast, that no, that wouldn't be necessary, but that he'd call a cab to take me anywhere I wanted to go, and I thought to myself, the night's still young, it's not even one yet, still time to fit in another john, but what about the clothes? They're yours, he said, mine? and he asked me again where I'd like to be taken, he insisted and I felt sorry for him, I couldn't just leave him like that and hitch up with another guy, not that night, at least, so I said I wanted to be dropped home, and he looked puzzled, home? don't you want to go out, meet your friends? you're so young, so lovely, and I mumbled, friends? no, no, I just want to go home, so he asked the security guard to hail a cab and he closed my hand round some folded-up notes, awkward as hell, and I didn't count them then, but it turned out it was exactly what we'd arranged, and then he opened the cab door and saw me inside, like a lady. He gave the driver my address and kissed the back of my hand, and stood there waving as the car pulled off and I watched him out the back window until he disappeared in the darkness of the street. I never saw him again. But whenever bad stuff happens, when they screw me over, like the son of a bitch who brought me to this motel and now wants me to do him and his two friends at the same time, a cock in my mouth, a cock in my pussy, and a cock in my ass, what do they think I am, for the love of god? but if I don't do what they want they'll beat the crap out of me, because they're already off their heads on coke and whiskey, and the bastard's just slapped me in the face, cutting my lower lip, so there's not much for it, they're going to gangbang me one way or another, but whenever shit happens I remember that day, Iguatemi mall, the do in Moema, that restaurant on Oscar Freire, a place these pricks have probably never been in, never been in, and never will, no never . . .

59. Knockout

That last right-hand jab sent him onto the ropes. Groggy, the implacable opponent, the ref's bowtie, the rolled-up sleeves of multicolored shirts around the ring, the crowd baying on its feet in the stands, everything spinning, the grease trickling down his nose, the gloves sucking on dangling hands, everything aswirl, he hadn't eaten since midday, when he had lunch at a bar on Sete de Abril, and his stomach and legs are reminding him of that now, his head light, arms like shipwrecks,

yes,

he didn't come down from Rio de Janeiro to win the fight, the agreement was to challenge and lose, make sure that the Brazilian middleweight champion ended the evening with his belt across his chest, and in return he'd earn enough to fill two months' worth of shopping carts, unemployed, the family put up at the brother-in-law's in Campo Grande and with things looking grim he took the call from Antenor, on the bus down from Itapemirim he watched the stars adorning the dark cave roof of night, breakfast (coffee and a roll) at the Tietê bus terminal, lunch (rolled beef, rice, and mashed potatoes) downtown, in the liquid blue afternoon, he wandered around, no place to go, dodging pickpockets, peddlers, cops, suits-and-ties, street bums, wasting shoe leather on the pissy streets, anxiety mounting, already missing the wife and the kids like crazy,

dizzy, weak-kneed,

turbid vision, muscles and bones splayed out on the deck, finally! the sweat gluing his face to the stretched green canvas, he was wishing it would end soon, the gym emptied out, the floodlights switched off, so he could have a shower and something to eat, then crash out on the reclining coach seat back to Rio, the kids, how'd it go, Dad? Not this time, he'd say, looking embarrassed, I need to train some more, then he'd fill up the supermarket cart with food and crap for the kids, yogurt, chewing gum, sweets, he might even give the wife a liter of Martini, which she loves, but never drinks, a bottle of Natu Nobilis for the brother-in-law, and a crate of beer for himself, he's earned it. Then back to the job hunt.

so

the opponent strutting, arms raised triumphantly to the four corners of the gym, they hugged briefly and he stepped down from the ring, Antenor said to him, hit the shower, I'll get the money, and he turned to the bouncer at the dressing room entrance, say, pal, where can I get some grub this time of night?

60. Jealousy

One of the biggest problems affecting any couple is jealousy. To eliminate this scourge, the cause of needless arguments that undermine the union, one should do the following: on a Thursday, buy a flask of perfume or cologne of your choosing. Bless it against jealousy by making the sign of the cross on the lid. Give the flask to the jealous partner, saying that you like the fragrance and would like him or her to wear it. As the liquid is gradually used up, the jealousy will disappear in equal measure.

61. Night

Coming in my direction, a girl, not even fifteen yet I'd say, her kinky hair chemically straightened and tied into a ponytail with a red elastic. Trim white dress, with embroidered flowers on the chest. Her feet, transparent plastic sandals, moving her about hawking mints, with a pretty pearly smile. Have you eaten, I ask? She hides her dark eyes and flashes her white teeth, her slim shoulders shrug. No, she says. I light up a smoke, drink down my coffee, and push the cup away. How much? I ask, and she replies, chirpily. Come on, let's get something to eat, I say, turning my back. I go into a newsstand, court some foreign titles, walk out into the chill night, cars gliding by on Paulista Avenue, side by side, What's your name? Marina, and yours? Humberto, we go into Habib's, Do you like Arabian fast food? We sit in silence, Eat, I say. Whatever you'd like. She devours kibbes (two), *sfihas* (two), a beirute sandwich, and some pizza (three slices). I watch her over the top of my newspaper: she eats stupidly, metaphysically. I get the check and say goodbye at the doorway, and she asks, And the mints? Don't you want some? I say nothing, light another smoke, Go home, go on, and she hides her dark eyes and we say goodnight. She walks a child's walk down the Portuguese stone sidewalk. At the crosswalk she intercepts a man, who's in a hurry, doesn't stop, waves her away, scurries on. She approaches a couple, the woman kneels down to chat to her; I stamp out a cig end on the ground, breathe in the crisp night air, and walk on beneath the marquee, where drunken bums pull up their cardboard blankets to sleep, some scrawny mongrels tear at the black rubbish sacks, some cabdrivers play thimblerig at an improvised rank, a woman peddles Indian incense, her baby asleep on the bench beside her, cars drive by, empty buses, closed subway stairways, a police car with sirens wailing, where's Marina? this malaise is never going to go away, this feeling of uselessness, Marina! Marina! and I walk on, mumbling, breathing in the suffocating belch of exhaust fumes.

62. The last time

I don't even remember what we fought about the last time, but I grabbed my stuff (I'd prepacked a leather bag with shirts, trousers, underwear, socks, toothbrush, toothpaste, dental floss, towels, soap, deodorant, disposable razor, shaving cream, in short, everything a man needs to get by on his own for a while . . . or forever. . . .)

then I got into a cab and stopped off at the first half-decent (or half-affordable) hotel I came across—

(that's not true, actually, I'd seen that hotel on other occasions and always figured I might need it someday, if only for a weekend break away from it all)

so I settled into my room, do you remember?

Friday night, Hotel Amazonas, Vieira
de Carvalho Avenue, the noise of the street below
an Italian restaurant on the ground floor
and an Arab fast-food joint,
cars,
buses,
down below,
on the side streets,
and I knew all about the hookers,
the kids smoking crack,
the two-bit hoods,
I knew the night,

And I lay down, but it wasn't relief I felt, or remorse, I don't know what it was, maybe I was missing home already,
I knew I'd miss the kids, with their pajamas thrown in a heap, running, all sweaty, round the tiny living room of our ridiculously tiny apartment, which you always complained about, saying
We've got to get out of here
get out of here
out
and I'd agree, I was working my ass off at the firm, but always in the red, always on overdraft, rolling credit card bills
and the kids holed up in that ridiculously tiny apartment with the sun exploding on the TV screen on weekends and both of us feeling guilty

the stressful life we lead in São Paulo
our rat-race incompetence
the kids
the genetic inheritance of our parents
me
you
and our phenomenal bust-ups:
at Sandra's first birthday party
at Boi na Lenha rotisserie
at Fabíola's preprimary leaving party
on that long weekend in São Pedro
over that Woody Allen film you didn't want to see
and the Harrison Ford flick I didn't want to watch
over your friends
and my friends
(and in the end I discovered a paradox:
intimacy strengthens a relationship
intimacy ruins a relationship)

I wouldn't be happy (or this happy) without the memory of
your naked body
your breasts
your thighs
your ass
I wouldn't be unhappy (or so unhappy)
intimacy is the death of a relationship
(see how I find it hard even to say the word . . . marriage?)
intimacy is the death of a relationship:
I wouldn't fart in front of any other woman

I wouldn't confess my smelly feet
my chilblains
my bad breath
my bad humor
my foibles
to any woman I was in love with

My god, and just to think that that was ten years ago! Ten years!

63. Our get-together

Paulo Sérgio Módena, at your service. São Paulo through-and-through, born and bred in Brás, thirty-eight years of age (though people say I look much younger, either out of cynicism or mockery, I'm not sure, though the blood tests are starting to show high cholesterol and triglycerides). I'm neither rich nor poor—I get by—and, if need be, if really pertinent, I have the tax returns to prove it (all PAYE); you can pull my bank, phone, tax records, I have nothing to hide, especially after nine draught beers. My car is always three years behind the posse. Small apartment in Perdizes (in Pompeia if you're buying), and I'm still paying the mortgage with Caixa Econômica Federal, with a florid, endless sum outstanding. Very, very single am I, at the moment anyway, though technically married, and encumbered with a teenage and therefore problematic son, the kind that will only wear black, has piercings down to his butt, likes heavy metal, dirty tennis shoes, adrenaline, video games, slang, kung fu, revolution, all that crap. I pay the alimony right on time, I'm responsible for his high school tuition and pocket money, which means that I couldn't remarry even if I wanted to because there's not a penny to spare. So all I have to offer the womenfolk is some good conversation and an honest fuck: sound cost-benefit there. The ex doesn't get in the way, but she doesn't help either. She remarried, to a nice guy, a mechanical engineer, who's polite when he answers the phone, but a little suspicious, which is stupid, seeing as myself and Guilherme's mother harbor a mutual if civilized loathing.

But I'm not here to expose myself warts-and-all, but rather the friends who join me tonight—ten thirty p.m.—at this table, strewn with knives, forks, cell phones, surrounded by voices, cars and buses, "mechanical music," lights, cigarette smoke, the smell of cooked fat, beer, and sweat. We've been coming here for the last four years. Before that we used a variety of establishments, and I could wax sociological about each and every one of them—the comings and goings of the Brazilian middle class over the course of the last fifteen years—but I'll spare the reader that particular wank. During this period we've been snobs—ah, Praça Vilaboim!; populists—the leg of lamb at Kinzle! a restaurant near the Palmeiras club ground; eccentric—ah, the cabbage salad at Bar das Putas! But now we have settled into that precarious balance called maturity. Too old to while away the night over unknown singer-songwriters at Café Paris; too broke to foot the bill after a month at All That Jazz; so it's beers and bar grub at the Galinheiro Grill: a sign of the times.

But we'll get to that in time. If anyone were to ask why our annual get-together falls on the ninth of May, I don't know if any of us could be bothered saying, but the date was picked sixteen years ago, and it's been my job ever since to rally the troops. Our group, a product of student militancy (toward the end of the dictatorship), is a mixed bunch, intellectually and socially, which, for some reason or other, came together to demand amnesty for political prisoners and then regrouped on the campaign for direct elections.

The founding members—reunited at the mega-demonstration in Vale do Anhangabaú—were myself, Paula Meirelles, Chico Almeida, Ana Beatriz, and Rodolfo. The following year there were two dozen of us, including university pals, wives, husbands, and others (boyfriends, girlfriends, kids, babies). Two years later it was back to the core group, except for Chico Almeida, whose car was pancaked by a truck on his way down to Curitiba for the theater festival. Then, at the fourth meeting, Paula insisted that we make a "blood pact," and now we no longer fear a dwindling of our numbers. Year after year, time chews its way through marriages, false friendships, and family hostilities, but we stand firm on the unshakable ground of old bonds with those who have seen us naked, who have deconstructed our histories, who know our pain, our solitude, our despair. Those gathered around this table are the flowers of "our time," the king's musketeers, and, seeing as I'm starting to get drunk, let me introduce them to you, with love and squalor, as good ol' J. D. Salinger would say.

Paula Meirelles—To my right, a relatively successful lawyer, forty-three years of age, although rather the worse for wear. We had a fling way back when. We met up again at the march for direct elections—Diretos Já—she was married at the time, so was I. Her husband owned an important law firm, I can't remember the name now, but he was super-famous, that guy, Turkish surname, and she was crazy about him . . . until he dumped her for a student of his. . . . That was the only year she didn't turn up, 1995. In 1996, though, she was back with bells on, though aged and fattened, packing a load on her butt, with crow's feet sprouting around her brown eyes, and prodigious with smokes and beers. She'd been left with almost nothing, because she'd put her career on hold to bring up the kids. When the husband suddenly filed for legal separation, she found herself at a crossroads. It was the loyalty of her kids that got her through, both of whom have good heads on them. Last year, the eldest dropped her off. He came in, face erupting in zits, and said a shy hello, very presentable and polite, he was like his mother's bodyguard, then disappeared. When it was time to head home, she called him from her cell phone and he was there within twenty minutes, honking outside in the street. I envied her. My son is a prehistoric creature who hates me and his mother. Paula's brightest quality is her upbeat attitude. I'd have married her, maybe, in the past, but not now. We get on well, she's the most interesting of the bunch. One of the few good-humored women I know.

Ana Beatriz—Journalist. Inconstant in every way. Neurotic, she chews her fingernails, even when she's relaxed. She considers herself ugly, even though she's not. Unspecified age—for the others, not me, cuz I've seen her ID. This one time she got hammered and I took her home. At the door to her apartment, in Aclimação, I opened her bag to look for the keys, and out fell three whole bunches of them, along with some foundation, lipstick, blusher, a hair clip, a pen, an old lottery ticket, a pack of condoms, a wallet, a health insurance card, a chocolate bar, a saint's medal, I don't know which one—I never was any good at identifying saints—some mints, an address book, and her ID, so I saw her age, thirty-seven, though the age lies. She could easily pass for thirty when she arrives at our get-together, or for forty-five when she leaves, reeking of cigs and beer, her hair a mess, her eyeliner running, eyes bulging, and that manic smirk (Rodolfo's diagnosis is hysteria). She considers herself a loser, never married, but she does have a daughter, "an independent production," though she never lived with her, as the kid was brought up by her parents in Jundiaí. I feel sorry for her. Sometimes I feel like doing her, but it would be too much trouble, she'd want something more serious, she already grabs onto whoever comes along just to avoid being alone. As the night wears on, the desperation mounts, she starts knocking back beer after beer and hitting on whoever happens to be beside her. It's Márcio this time, and she's already starting to hug him, making the fool drool.

RODOLFO—Psychoanalyst (Freudian, let it be said), trained at PUC. He's an angst-ridden soul, an inveterate smoker, voracious reader, cultured, sophisticated, a wine connoisseur (especially wine of the Portuguese variety), with various articles published in journals and books, he specializes in adolescent traumas. He's been married three times with absolutely no luck. I met the last two, but not the first. He had a daughter with Marina, the middle wife, but it seems the girl's got problems. They live in the US, and the ex is always on his back for something, higher alimony for example, and she's brought him to court more than once. He can't even bear to hear her name. (Once, while looking for a book on the bookstands at Fnac, he got into a tangle with this blonde who was looking for the same title. They started laughing, each picked up a copy of said book, paid, and went down to the cyber café, and when they found a table he said I'm Rodolfo, psychoanalyst, and she said Marina, psychoanalyst, and he nearly choked on his doughnut and spilled his latte on his trousers. Later, analyzing the scene, he decided to tear up the calling card she'd kindly given him.) The third wife, the present one, I'm not sure, is studying for a master's degree in education at USP. She's stuck up, with the oily black hair of someone who's not big on showering, and she's got surly but strangely youthful eyes that make her look as if she's always scanning for the perpetrators of as yet unknown crimes. Rodolfo fights a losing battle against dandruff.

PIERRE—Assiduous member for the last four years, he's a failed doctor, the kind that works for the public health system, running from center to center. He's married to Linda, whose name—the cruel irony—translates as "lovely." We met him back in our student years. He was president of the Center for Academic Medicine. Shy and reserved—I never could understand how he got mixed up in politics, which, for him, is vital. He is still a fervent communist, a member of the PC do B, the Brazilian Communist Party, and a fan of João Amazonas. A complete radical, he's one of the few of us who hasn't settled. He won't sit anywhere near Márcio, from whom he even refused to accept a CD of Albanese music (Márcio said he'd bought it in Tirana, which was a lie, he later confessed he only said that to get back at Pierre, but it backfired, Pierre was green with envy, felt humiliated, and hasn't said a word to him since). Pierre never has any money, so he'll make for the restroom just as the bill arrives in the hope that someone will pick up his tab. He has three kids, who inherited their mother's kung-fu features, and he's intent on turning the household into a cell of the PC do B. Linda is more down to earth. Like all women, she worries about what her kids will have to eat the following day, while Pierre swans about with his cardboard folder full of newspaper clippings on the corruption in city hall and the state and federal governments. And whenever he has one too many—which, being a pussy, is usually about the fourth glass—he becomes a real pain in the ass, full of flaming discourse one minute and rolled up like an armadillo the next, glaring out at the rest of us from his bunker of silence.

MÁRCIO—I don't know his surname. He wasn't part of the original group. He's a later addition. It was Angélica (great tits), from Chico Almeida's circle, who introduced him. She turned up one day with Márcio in tow, and he's been coming ever since, though Angélica stopped. Ana Beatriz says she married up and has no more time for bullshit. Márcio is an arrogant dick of unspecified profession. Since he started coming he's mentioned several different lines of activity, but Rodolfo thinks he's just a ruffian. Paula reckons he deals in used cars. I don't know. He's suspicious, though. In bygone times I would have sworn blind he was a regime snitch infiltrated into our midst. He's always in a good mood, and tells some pretty bawdy jokes (he tells them well, too, the schmuck, especially ones about the Portuguese and parrots), and they get dirtier and dirtier the drunker he gets. He's got money. He's been to Europe a few times (or so he says) and he hits on every chick in sight. He's been out with Ana Beatriz (definitely) and he's tried it on with Paula every which way, but she's been around and knows the type. He always brings some memento back from his trips, for someone or other ("I was in Paris and thought I'd bring you this wine . . ."). He even gave me a present once (a white and blue tile on corkwood backing, with a scene of Lisbon painted on it, would you give me a break!). I'd love to know what he really does, though. He talks about the coup of '64, but where was he during the dictatorship? He's a reactionary, he probably votes right wing. I'm getting old. . . . In the past, a douche like that would have been met with irony and sarcasm, but today, we just accept him . . . the way he is. . . . What the heck.

Marília—A contemporary of mine from the literature department. She had a hard time getting through university. Her father, a lathe operator, and her mother, a washerwoman. Her family was huge, seven siblings, all packed into this little house over in Jardim São Norberto, in São Bernardo do Campo. She gave classes at various private schools to pay her fees, so she never had any money to buy books, which she had to borrow from the library at USP or from the Mário de Andrade. She married this dullard, a miller I think, a friendly enough sort, who she reckoned she could "redeem" from ignorance. But their intellectual disparity spoke the louder. She wanted to be independent, but he wanted her home minding the kids. Their misunderstandings turned to arguments, and the arguments to physical aggression. She reported him to the cops once, but then pulled the complaint. She felt sorry for him. He hit the drink hard and she realized that she was doing him no good, and that the decent thing to do was end the marriage, which she did, after only three years. All she came away with was their daughter, and a life to rebuild.

She worked her ass off to study French, then did a master's degree before applying for and winning a scholarship to do a doctorate in literary theory at University Paris III. She returned, got back on her feet, and now she's doing nicely. She published a collection of short stories a few years ago, and we all went to the launch at Livraria Cultura. The book's not up to much, but she's lecturing in a number of universities, earning good money, and her daughter's doing well. She's a loyal friend, conciliating and smiley, but down in her cellar she's got a husband drinking himself crazy in the dingiest dives of São Bernardo.

We've had three losses over the last fifteen years (besides Chico Almeida, dead en route to Curitiba):

Oswaldão—Went back to Belo Horizonte for good, taking his wife and two kids with him. He couldn't stand the life here in São Paulo, so he sold up and left. Every now and then he calls up complaining about stuff. Seems one of the kids has a drug problem.

Silveira—Killed himself three years ago. He was broke. Every venture he tried went bust: a restaurant, a publishing house, a video rental store, an esoteric products store. He was single and had some unresolved issues with his sexuality.

Lincoln—Killed during a break-in at his house in Vila Romana.

64. Crates

"There's this pile of wooden crates, see, which the guys leave out to be loaded up early in the morning. I was in my spot, quiet, listenin' to the radio; it's nice, late at night, to listen to some country music, it reminds me of back home, with the chickens pecking in the yard, the cocks tearing at the dirt with their long claws, the cattle mooing, and then I heard this huge bang, sounded like a power box exploding, boom! it was dark, real dark, so I didn't see nothin', I just heard the noise, so then I did what they told me to do when something weird happens, if I saw something strange. . . ."

"We were comin' back from Perus, from a pal's crib, so we came on foot, because the buses had stopped runnin', so we was walkin' and talkin', see? Then we saw this stack of crates, and we said, that's weird, then Skeley says, let's knock 'em over! and Ziquinho said, no way, bro, you just gonna get us in shit, but then Skeley and Ratsy went runnin' off at them crates, and Skeley jump-kicks the stack, which wobbles but don't fall, so Ratsy rams it good 'n' hard, and then there was this loud noise, boom! it was funny at first, but then all I saw was Ratsy on the ground, and Ziquinho on the ground, and I thought they was playin' me, but then I hightailed after Skeley, from the noise of it, I was sure we was toast, and then I found out that Ratsy'd bought it, that the bullet got him straight in the eye, and that Ziquinho was here in hospital, in intensive care, all messed up, so I came over here to see him, but that's all I know, sir, I don't know nothin' more than that. . . ."

65. List (3)

Aretha Purrrr—Delicious, up for anything, with accessories, total sex.

Arlete Blonde—Lusty, big tits, titjob, and anal queen. Does lesbians, men, women.

Astrid Gaucha—Sculptural blonde, foxy, dirty, complete. Him/her/couple.

Babalu 19 Years Old—Blonde, green eyes, uninhibited, complete, anal, oral, vaginal, sixty-nine, active, passive.

Baianinha—Lusty all positions, anal, totally safe.

Bella Transvestite—Active, passive, hygienic space, discreet, with buzzer.

Bia Mineira + Girlfriend—Hot and horny, wild in every position.

Cowboy & Bob—23, third-level education, 5ft 10/6ft, redhead/dark-haired. Girls only.

César—For women and couples. Come play out your fantasies. Confidential and discreet.

Dany—Him? Her? Come dabble in the pleasures and mysteries of total sex. House calls.

Discreet MILF—Uninhibited, insatiable, will fulfill your fantasies with sex toys, costumes, erotic massage, lesbians, men, women.

Horny MILF—Black, beautiful, attends clientele from her residence.

Married MILF 38 Years Old—Blonde, large breasts, does oral, total, anal, plays with sex toys.

66. Street

There he is again, on the corner of Bela Cintra and Alameda Jaú, standing on the sidewalk, eyes fixed on two small, dimly lit windows stuck in between the water tower and the terrace, just over the concrete lintel above the top floor of the art nouveau building. Night nestles in the tree boughs, a damp chill slinks across the irregular asphalt.

There he is again, with that same disgusting beard, a tangle of dark and white strands, encrusted with crumbs of bread and husks of rice, his cotton shirt of uncertain color, riddled with holes, old jeans held in place by a piece of rope, toeless shoes, a paper bag from a boutique in his left hand, black fingernails.

He doesn't like memories, he wanders the streets as if in a labyrinth. Each, surprisingly, surprises him. What good are memories? Times . . . spaces . . . nothing . . . Memory reconstructs nothing, it just rekindles old pain. . . . What we did, what we failed to do. The worst part is that the mind . . . Slowly, his varicose legs shunt him up the hill . . . slowly . . . very slowly . . . the doorman watches him warily . . . the lad from the bakery, crook in hand, just about to bring down the shutters, regards him as he passes . . . he kicks at a mongrel that insists on sniffing the pavement, his toe jabs between its skinny ribs . . . what if, you never know, he used to live in that building . . . the shame . . .

The baby threw itself into grandma's lap and vanished with her to Itapecerica da Serra. So lovely, smiley, rosy, enormous. A Vicentini! The mother-in-law, beside herself, was shouting in the middle of the maternity corridor, A Vicentini! They came from northern Paraná, down south, smallholders sent to ruin by the frost, and went to work in the fields in the region of Avaré. Tired out, the father-in-law decided to try his luck in the capital, and found a job as a caretaker at the building now in view. Always thrifty and economical, he put aside enough money to buy the house he most likely still lives in today, in Itapecerica da Serra. Though he still had some years left in him, he decided to retire to make room for his son-in-law, his replacement, who was engaged to marry his daughter and had only a few unstable shifts at a paint factory. At least as caretaker they'd have a roof over their head, in an excellent location, right at the heart of the city; they could save up to buy a place of their own for their old age, without having to depend on their children. The syndic accepted the recommendation, though he was sad to see the caretaker go, and with the money from his guarantee fund, the son-in-law managed to furnish the caretaker's apartment and pay for the wedding party, much appreciated by the relatives.

From the very first day he set foot in the cobblestone entrance, he immersed himself in his function, devoting all his energies to that building, morning, noon, and night, eager to eclipse his father-in-law's well-deserved fame. He had no shortage of skills, many of which his elder had lacked, as they are not acquired with a hoe on a field. Things he'd had neither the time nor the wherewithal to learn, such as reading and writing, his son-in-law mastered to the point of ascending to the pulpit to read from the scriptures at the House of Blessings, the church they all attended every Sunday. Arts, these, at which the elder could make but rudimentary stabs, the evidence of nocturnal attempts to tame the wild hand, a prerequisite for making the electoral register.

Yet this had been no obstacle to his raising his three children in the knowledge of the scriptures and the word of God, in fact, one of his sons became a pastor, now toiling as a missionary in Mozambique, while the eldest married a church brother and moved to Francisco Mourato. The youngest, of course, grew up in the building, where she was well liked by all. With her blond head pushing at the safety netting on the windows, she used to watch the children in the playground below, climbing on the jungle gym, swinging on the swings, bouncing up and down on the seesaws, breaking a sweat on the volleyball court, or playing basketball, or indoor football, playing dodgeball, riding tricycles, bicycles, and scooters. As the daughter of staff, she couldn't mix with the other girls in the elevator, all so prettily dressed. Sometimes she was given outgrown clothes, which she tried in vain to squeeze into, but she was too big, too pudgy, a freckled, pink Italian peasant. She discovered boys when she hit the teenage years, but they only had eyes for their own. At night, her blond mane blowing in the wind, she'd lean on the windowsill and watch the guys and gals in the playground below, little red fireflies in the dark corners, necking in the sports courts and behind the pillars of the hall.

When she met her future husband, at Sunday service at the House of Blessings, she was under no illusions, she was an aging maiden of well-restrained joys. And so it went, the wedding ball, the moving out—it was strange for her: the same-old space was not the same-old space, but she had no time to dwell on such things, as pregnancy—for the honor and glory of the Lord—brought morning sickness and dizzy spells, swollen legs and mood swings, and her bouts of sadness and happiness swept away all other concerns. The hard part was climbing the two flights of seven steps apiece from the top floor elevator to the caretaker's apartment, short of breath and lugging that enormous belly, her lower back a blaze of pain, its tongues lashing down to her legs.

There were nights the devil, with whom her husband wrestled with every misstep at the building's gate or halls, prowled her thoughts, the nullity that was she, dressed in silence, where were the boys and girls of the building? important young men and women, she masked her doubts, the devil, nothing, what was that? nothing, observing the lights of far-off helicopters, nothing, Daniel so lovely, so smiley, so rosy, enormous, sleeping loudly in his crib, the pacifier half popping from the corner of his mouth, the rumble of traffic down below, the fumes of burnt gasoline, Daniel, what will become of Daniel? she often thought, the devil, if, by chance the hand of God, if the hand of God should, should the hand of God.

Then came the explosion, the underused kaleidoscope in her head spilled its multicolored shards across the floor, shimmering in the sitting room, the kitchen, the bathroom, an intolerable agony, there's a rat, she pointed at her nape, a rat gnawing my thoughts, scratching my notions. Dr. Porto, from the fifteenth floor, came in all sleepy-headed and said it was best to send her to the neurological department at Clínicas Hospital, get her over there, I'll put a call through to a student of mine who's on duty tonight. They left her at the ER door, in a wheelchair, in the care of a nurse, her mouth all crooked, her eyes sunken, he came rushing out of the elevator and the baby's cries rolled down the stairs from the apartment door. He rang his mother-in-law, who called her son-in-law in Francisco Mourato, who came to pick her up in Itapecerica da Serra and drove her to the hospital, where they found her already dead, of an aneurism, though not one of them had the courage to ask what the hell that meant, what was this disease that had taken their wife, daughter, sister, not one had the courage, none the initiative.

The apartment could only remember the baby's cries, the wife's slippered footsteps, the little radio, the hushed conversations they enjoyed, and faith lost her in that silence. At night, he walked out into the fresh shadows of the trees, moths in rings around the streetlights, flies in the stifling gob of car and bus and truck fumes, he stepped into a bar on Augusta, the devil, his mouth empty of words, and he ordered a shot and a pack of cigarettes, then a beer, and he crawled back up to his apartment late that night, as a seven-year wagon chugged on without him and the walls of the House of Blessings came tumbling down.

And his body liked to dance among the liquor's flames, soak itself in the wet vulva of beer, to disappear in the fog of fagsmoke. The devil took him under his wing. Throughout the day, he dribbled temptation by scouring for the source of the leak staining the bathroom ceiling on the tenth floor, or resurfacing the barbecue, or cleaning the pool, or scrubbing down the garage floor, or listening to the complaints of the old woman on the first, or the gossip of the lady on the eighth. But the streetlights lit up his loneliness in the evenings, and it squirmed toward him between the furniture, ringing the bell to rouse the devil of his tattered soul slumped on the sofa, eyes blank, the TV on mute, his dry lips pursed around an empty bottle.

But everything ends, and some things end all the faster the greater is the desire to see them end.

He fell off the couch onto the floor, jamming his arms under his back. His head was pounding. He rubbed the sleep from his eyes and checked the time, eleven thirty, Raimundo, calling from the front door, nervous, whispering, Fred, from the ninth, the gym guy, yeah, he's trying to bring in that Jerry punk again, the troublemaker, the one the syndic barred from the building, what do I do? The caretaker stumbled into the entranceway, head pounding, and said, Fred, the lad can't come in. We have orders, from the syndic. In a growl, eyes wide, Fred, who's this redneck to keep me out of the building? I want to see who's gonna stop me, neither you nor that nigger there's gonna lock me out, fuckin' hillbilly, dumbass nigger, try and stop me, I'm comin' in, open the gate, or I'll jump over and fuck you two up, open it, pussy! Do what I tell you! What do I do? Open it? No, if this punk thinks he can make us drop our pants just by shouting he's got another thing coming. You don't scare me, kid, you don't scare me. Oh no? So I'm goin' in there right now and I'm gonna fuck you two up. Fred, a jujitsu fighter, jumped over the gate—Raimundo tried to stop him but was sent reeling into the rose bed with a kick—and he went straight for the buzzer and the caretaker tried to intercept him with a pool cue, but he was laid out with a chop. A group formed, watching terrified, passive, as Fred headed back toward the gate, yelling, I'm gonna fuck you up, nigger, son of a bitch, I'm gonna fuck you up!

He lay there, facedown, his body aching, the grass cushioning his face, no will to even move. He went to the police to file a complaint, Raimundo wouldn't go, he was afraid he'd lose his job. The duty sergeant came straight out with it, It's a waste of time, the lad's got family, money behind him. And you've got no witnesses, not one.

The syndic was pretty good about the whole thing, he said, unfortunately, there was nothing he could do, but he paid everything that was due, and a month on top, I'll sort that out later with the other residents, he said, with a smile. So he grabbed a paper supermarket bag and packed a change of clothes and hit the streets. One day he realized he'd drunk all the money and that he'd lost that white shirt somewhere, the one with blue lettering on the pocket that read *Jardim das Palmeiras Apartments Wilson Caretaker*. He couldn't remember where.

67. Insomnia

shit, things to do tomorrow, the brakes, oil change, do you wanna dance? Party, maria aparacida albino, blonde, sleepyhead, hot sun, the country house, sand pit, gravel, goal, sandals for posts, school group flávia dutra pombo river, lower vila teresa versus upper vila teresa, maria rita, maria rita, classified ad, looking for maria rita, jardim neighborhood, shantytown, fields of brazil, dust, mud, they're over there on the pitch playing ball, dinim's in the slammer, he's in shit, turned hood, matinee at cine edgard, lend me your student card? rain rains, wet air, flood, snakes, guavas, mangoes, pellets, died on the riverbank, a girl of fifteen, shot in the ear, did you hear that? the gunshot, let's go! slumped in the sitting-room armchair, the blood oozing, dripping onto the carpet, the eyes staring at me, asking me, the wall clock reading half-past four, the walls need a lick of paint, the cracks, change the lightbulb in the living room, wooden floor, is the cell phone on? the door locked? The river, the rivulet, the waterfall, a dead mule stinks, sabiá bridge, ricardo eloped with virginia, off down the dirt road, shit, virginia sure was pretty, but she never even noticed me, my father turned up just as the boy was about to suck my cock, bicycles, broken glass, my torn foot, blood, vision clouded, stitches, arm raised up, yep, it's broken, took a tumble, a pike in the mango brush, I'm gonna fall, gonna, margarine or butter? broken arm, football, a cross floats in, isaias gets a head to it, straight into the left-hand corner, I love you, I love you, marcílio is screwing me over, he wants to take me down, I'm gonna lose my job, what? What? carla, mellifluous voice behind me, negative, negative, get the money from the bank and buy a house for my mother, she'll be so happy, and you? and you? she's waiting for me, but when the time comes I can't get it up, maybe if I used viagra? The prozac is knocking me out, more and more, garlic bread, cinnamon bread, sliced bread, french bread, cheese bread, bread bread, cheese cheese, felipe never called, have I been a good father? Have I? you're a great guy, really, super, mega, hyper, everyone's frozen you out, they're not going to do anything for the moment, but when you least expect it, nail clippers, marilza got rid of the nail clippers, sirens, police? Fire brigade? Police, someone goes by shouting corinthians, corinthians, coringão, uh oh, uh oh, fireworks, they're going to stab you in the back, unemployment figures going down, in brasília at seven p.m., the guarani, a tango, a samba, a bolero, national radio, I wanted to let reinaldo know that mom is leaving on the fifteenth and he'll have to pick her up, the neighbor, 43, hot, a model? an actress? a model-and-actress? luiz, luiz, your maintenance fee is in arrears, four months due, and, lights shine on the wall, see this hammock, look at this hammock, that's the real deal from fortaleza, you could, you know, sympathy is practically love, submarine, if you stay with me I'll make it snow in são paulo, the three little pigs, a poster hung on the sitting-room wall, the big bad wolf eternally stewing in a pot on the stove, eyes bulging, marcela tipped you off, they're trying to get rid of you, they're going to fuck you over, the night guard's whistle, the birds in the trees, the last bus pulls into the garage, silence, voices in the elevator shaft, laughter, a car stops outside the building, someone gets out, says goodnight, the door slams, the car pulls off, the korean's a doctor? Is the korean a doctor? the syndic is renovating his apartment with money from the building's maintenance fund, so they say, then they say a lot of things, the lawyer from number 13 always brings in hookers, the camera in the elevator, you can't clean your teeth with your tongue anymore, can't scratch your balls anymore, can't covet your neighbor's wife anymore, the girl from 73, seems she works at café-photo, recognized me, looked away, embarrassed, green eyes, very expensive, otherwise I'd use her, green eyes, natural blonde, great body, party in the building next door, techno-pop, fever, put your hand on my forehead, is it a fever? yeah, forty-five drops, orange tea, cover up, hand brushes back the fringe, you're burning up, wrap your legs round daddy's trunk, buy some soda, buy a bike, buy some corn biscuits, buy some sweets, head rests on my sister's lap, mud-stained face, car radio, '60s rock CD, the shame of it, I still miss the smokes, when I'm old, I'll take up smoking again, stop, please, for me, one day we'll meet up in paris, in the quartier latin, adeus, carlton, goodbye, marlboro, I miss the smoke in my lungs, that sensation of pleasure, that light torpor, it gives you cancer, it stinks, from every pore, your clothes reek, your breath, stop, they're stabbing you in the back, they're going to pull the rug from under your feet, they're going to fuck you over, my uncle I'm going to get rid of this kid's asthma once and for all, I'm gonna throw him in the cold water of pombo river, I come out purple cold, shaking, I love you, paris, they're stabbing you in the back, techno-pop, the night guard's whistle, the

68. Menu

Cocktail

Mini-quiche with dried tomato and courgette
Apricot with Gruyère cheese and nuts
Chinese pastel
Liver pâté à cigarettes
Palm heart pasty

Starter

Fresh asparagus salad with lobster medallion and endives
Rustic potatoes with olive oil and herbs
Pâté feuilletée and pear sauce
Shitake pie with capers
Smoked salmon and pancake
Salmon roe
Chilled French leek soup
Salmon in watercress and passion fruit

Main Course

Ham and endive risotto

Dessert

Marzipan and chocolate tart
Coconut mille-feuille
Strawberry meringue
Cream of passion-fruit ice cream with caramel topping
Fresh fruit salad with cinnamon

{—Woman . . . hey, woman . . .
—What?
—Did you hear that?
—What?
—Did you hear it?
—What?
—Shh-shh . . .
—What?
—Did you hear that?
(pause)
—Sounds . . . sounds like someone's groaning . . .
—Yeah . . .
—Good God!
— Shh-shh . . . keep it down!
—Aren't we going to help?
—Are you nuts?
—But . . . he's right there . . . at the door. . . .
—Quiet!
—Oh dear Lord!
(pause)
—Must have been stabbed . . . by the looks of it . . .
—And we're just going to sit here and do nothing?
—Do what? Do what, woman? Shush . . . What if there's someone else out there? Hiding?
(pause)
—It's stopped. . . .
—What has?
—Seems it's stopped . . .
—What has?

—The groaning . . .

(pause)

—Yes . . . it has . . . let's go take a look?

—No!

—Why not?

—Because . . . because there might still be somebody out there . . . Then what? Let's just go to bed. . . . Go on . . . roll over . . . roll over and go to sleep. . . . In the morning . . . tomorrow . . . We'll find out all about it tomorrow. . . . Go to sleep . . . off you go. . . .}

About the Author

© Marcia Zoet

Born in 1961, in Cataguases, Brazil, Luiz Ruffato grew up in a poor migrant family. He worked, among other jobs, as a textile worker and a turner-mechanic, and he studied journalism. In 2001, he debuted with a novel, *There Were Many Horses*. Praised for its vivid depiction of the urbanization of the author's hometown, São Paulo, the book revolutionized Brazilian literature, winning critical acclaim and a number of prizes, including the Brazilian National Library's Machado de Assis Award and the APCA Award for best novel. A jury of literary critics from the newspaper *O Globo* proclaimed the book—which has now been translated into German, Spanish (in Argentina and Colombia), French, and Italian, and also published in Portugal—to be one of the ten best Brazilian books of recent decades.

About the Translator

Anthony Doyle was born in Dublin, Ireland, where he took a Bachelor's degree in literature and philosophy and a master's degree in philosophy. He has been living in São Paulo, Brazil, since 2000. He translates fiction, nonfiction, and poetry. He is the author of the children's book *O Lago Secou* (Companhia das Letras, 2012).